Fisherman's Fog

by
James H. Pierce

1663 LIBERTY DRIVE, SUITE 200
BLOOMINGTON, INDIANA 47403
(800) 839-8640
WWW.AUTHORHOUSE.COM

Even though Red and Jim and the lake do really exist, all other characters and places in this story and its content are fictional.

© 2005 James H. Pierce. All Rights Reserved.

No part of this book may be reproduced, stored in a retrieval system, or transmitted by any means without the written permission of the author.

First published by AuthorHouse 08/05/05

ISBN: 1-4208-7091-2 (sc)

*Printed in the United States of America
Bloomington, Indiana*

This book is printed on acid-free paper.

It was a very cool late September morning, in a quiet little resort town up in Northern Wisconsin. The sun had not started to rise as of yet this morning as two fishermen prepared themselves to hit the lake and try to catch a few fish. They had packed their cooler with a few sandwiches and drinks for the day, because they knew once they got out on the lake they would not return until the sun was starting to set that evening. Red and Jim loved being out on the water and the peace that it brought to both of them. It didn't matter if the fish were biting or not, it was just sitting out there telling stories and laughing about old times. Red was the oldest of the two fishermen, but Jim was just a couple of years behind him. Red had worked many years and was now retired and had all the time he wanted to fish back home where he lived in Southern Illinois. However, Jim was still working toward his retirement and would take off a few weeks a year so they could head up north to get away.

As they left the cabin this morning, they noticed a heavy fog all across the lake. They knew this was going to be a problem getting started, but had decided to take it slow as they departed from the dock. Red was driving the boat and told Jim who was sitting up front to keep his eyes open for anything in the water. Jim shouted back, "AY Captain!" As if they were a couple of pirates on a ship at sea. Red was known for shouting out while cruising the waters things like, "Arrrr we are hunting the great white musky!" This would always make Jim laugh no matter how many times he had heard it before. This morning was very different, because as they made their way across the lake the fog seemed to get thicker and thicker until they found themselves sitting dead in the water. They could no longer even see a foot in front of the boat.

Red could hardly see Jim sitting in the front of the boat and said, "How far do you think we have gone?"

Jim hesitated for a moment and answered, " I am not really sure Red, I know we have gone quite a ways, but I cannot see the trees or shoreline to make anything out."

They both agreed it would be smart to sit and wait it out until the sun came up a bit more to burn the fog off the water. Normally that wouldn't take very long but this morning would turn out to be much different. The fog was so thick you couldn't even see the sun in the sky and the wind was as calm as they had ever seen it this time of the morning. They had both commented about how calm the lake had become as they both sat quietly listening for anything that may be coming toward them on the lake. The last thing they wanted was for another boat to come piercing through the fog and broad side them sitting still in the water. This was a very eerie feeling sitting out there in the middle of the lake not being able to see anything at all while the fog closed in around them, thicker and thicker as the morning went on.

They had sat out there for two and half hours now and they had noticed how the sounds that had carried across the lake had slowly faded away until the normal sounds that you would hear were gone. No more voices carrying across the water, no motors trying to start, just perfectly quiet. It was then that Jim looked up into the sky and noticed ever so slightly he could see the sun as it tried to pierce its way through the thick layer of fog. He pointed it out to Red and they both agreed that it looked as if the fog was beginning to lift, as the out line of trees along the shore started to appear as well.

They sat there patiently waiting for the fog to lift enough to find their bearings, but as it lifted they noticed they were a little confused about where they were located on the lake. They had been coming here for many years and had been to every part of the lake, but nothing looked familiar to either one of them. All of the cabins and homes and resorts that had been built along the shoreline were gone, as if they had vanished.

Red looked at Jim and said, "Do you recognize anything here?"

Jim always took pride in the fact that he knew this lake so well, answered, "Yes, I recognize the bend and cove up ahead but I don't understand, all the cabins are missing that were always there. It looks as if they were never there at all, the trees have not been cleared and the shoreline is undisturbed."

Red, with a puzzled look on his face replied, "How can this be possible? We are on the same lake that we have been coming to for many years and we have watched as all of these changes and homes have been built."

Jim said, " I don't know Red, but I think someone needs to pinch us both, because I think maybe we never woke up this morning and we are both dreaming. It was then that Jim noticed what looked like a man standing on the far shoreline and pointed him out to Red.

Red decided right then and there that he was going to find out just what the hell was going on around here. He turned, fired up the motor and started flying across the lake, while the man stood and stared at them as they came closer. You could almost see the confusion and fear in his eyes as they came closer and closer to the shore where he was standing. Before they could hit the shore the man turned and ran as fast as he could, as if he had seen a ghost or an alien space ship or something. When they arrived at shore the man was long gone and had left everything behind with signs that he had been staying there for quite sometime. His fishing gear was lying on the bank and looked as if it was as primitive as could be, a straight stick with twine tied to the end and what looked like a hook bent of wire. It was something that looked like you would have used a hundred years ago. The two of them figured he was a homeless man living in the woods doing the best he could with what he could make on his own and never gave it another thought. Further up into the woods was the shelter that he had built for a roof over his head and it was clear to both of them that he had been staying there for quite some time. Everything there seemed so very old but yet not in some strange way, as if it was old to them but had not seemed to age as most things do in time.

They decided to hang around for a while to see if the man would return, but that never happened. After several hours had passed, they both decided it was time to get back into the boat and head back where they were staying at the location of the resort. They jumped into the boat and fired the motor up and shot across the lake like a jet. The further they traveled the more they realized things were very different before. The shore line looked the same, but there was nothing but trees, no cabins, no resorts, not even another boat on the lake. The only choice they had was to try to find their way back to the camp, where they had seen someone already and hoped to see him again, so they could make some kind of sense of all of this.

For the next several days they stayed at the camp, going out to fish in the boat during the day to get food to eat. Red cast his line out into the water and just like that a walleye hit and took the bait. When he pulled it in to the boat, he couldn't help but notice it was the biggest and best looking walleye he had ever caught. Just as Jim was trying to reel in one on his line as well, they realized it was another magnificent fish. They couldn't help but notice how much better the fishing here was now, than anytime they could remember. After a discussion in the boat they had decided it was because the area was so undisturbed and natural. Nothing was like it was when they left in the boat that foggy morning, cabins lining the shore and boats normally scrabbling all about the lake. This was much more peaceful, something they both enjoyed very much, being the outdoors men that they were.

One of the things they couldn't help but notice back at the camp was, it didn't look like the man who had lived there was alone when he left. There were clear signs that he had a woman along with him, by the clothes and things that were also left behind. They very well could have been a husband and a wife, if marriage was an option here and now. They tried to not disturb their belongings anymore than they needed to, trying to figure out who they were and where they might have gone. They built their own shelter near by to sleep and get out of the weather if it decided to turn bad. The nights around these parts can get a little chilly this time of year and they both knew that. They both knew it was only a matter of days or weeks before the snow would start to fly and their plans were to be long gone before that ever happened. They were also wondering if someone was searching for them by now, since they never returned to the cabin. Surely someone was wondering where they were.

The two of them went out everyday scouting the lake looking for any sign of human life, but found no one anywhere. All they knew was the lake was surrounded by trees and they couldn't see beyond them. Somewhere there had to be someone out there other than the man they saw on the shore the first day. They took turns yelling out for someone to answer, but there was never a reply. Day after day they returned to the camp to find no one had returned, not even to gather their things and then run off again. They were both beginning to get a little more than just concerned, and neither one of them could come up with a reasonable answer for what had happened. Once again the only thing they could do was try to wait it out and see if someone would come along to answer their questions. Nightfall was coming on quickly so they rustled up a fire with the lighter Red had in his pocket that he used to smoke his hand rolled cigarettes. They then cooked their fish and filled their bellies and then decided to call it a night and try again tomorrow. They decided that tomorrow they would venture further up into the woods for signs of life or a cabin. They snuffed out the fire and faded off to sleep to end another very confusing but peaceful day.

Sometime late in the night while they both were sleeping, they were awaked by the sounds of something rustling through the camp. Red jumped up and lit a homemade torch that he had made. He was hoping it was the man who returned to collect his belongings, but it was not, it was a bear that had smelled the fish that they had cooked and had decided he was hungry too. Now he was standing on his back two feet looking at Red with the torch in his hand and let out one of those bone shaking growls. Jim scurried over to the other shelter and grabbed two cooking pans that the man had left behind and started banging them together to make as much noise as he could before the bear made a move for Red. The bear dropped down to all fours and took off running into the woods, the loud noises did the trick and now the bear was gone. Red's heart was racing and so was Jim's, now it was going to be hard to try to get some sleep. Red snuffed out the torch and neither of them said a word about it, they just laid down and tried to go back to sleep.

As they laid there in the dark, Jim started to laugh, and Red asked, "What do you think is so funny?"

Jim answered, "It was the look on your face when the bear stood up and walked toward you, all I could see was your face because you had the torch right there. You looked as if you were going to take him on, but I think you might have had your hands full this time old buddy."

Red laughed out loud and said, "You know you are right, I never even gave it a thought until now, but you were right. Besides, it wouldn't be the first time I got my butt kicked, at least I was going to go down fighting."

Jim said, " I think next time we might want to avoid the fight because we are going to have a hard time finding medical help out here wouldn't you say?"

Red still laughing replied, "Yes I guess you are right, goodnight!"

Jim mumbled goodnight and they both laid there trying to get some sleep and all through the rest of the night every little noise seemed to wake one of them up. They wondering if the bear would return, but he did not.

Morning finally came and they were both awake, waiting for the sunlight to arrive. Today they would venture deep into the woods looking for any signs of life. They packed the fish that the bear never found and set out to get some answers. They realized they needed to keep in mind that they only wanted to venture far enough to be able to have time to return to the camp before sunset. After all, so far this was the only place they had seen anyone since they had arrived, and could only hope that someday this person would return. They had enough gas in the boat to make several more trips from one end of the lake to the other, but so far that seemed to be unproductive. So now they felt venturing deep into the woods was just another attempt they had to try.

After walking several hours and marking their path back to the camp, they had still never seen a sign of human life anywhere at all. There was plenty of wildlife and tracks but none were from people. Jim decided it would be a good time for them to place a couple of snares to try to catch some game and they could check them on their way back to the camp if they found nothing as they continued. They made a few small game snares from small rope they had taken from the boat and they were hopeful they would not be eating fish again tonight. They were both getting a little tired of eating fish everyday. They continued walking through the woods marking their path, until the sun slid half way across the sky. They knew then it was time to turn back, if they were to make it back before dark. On their way back they were very happy to see that they had caught two rabbits in the snares that they had set. They were both very happy to see they would be having rabbit for dinner tonight. Red told Jim if he would clean them, he would cook them up and they both agreed that was fair enough. After not finding any help all day, it was at least nice to have something go right.

They sat by the fire and ate their rabbits as they talked about everything that had happened since they came out of the fog. Jim and Red both agreed that after all the years they had been coming here, this was the best time they had ever had, even though they were lost and didn't know how they were going to ever get back home. They sat there and talked almost all night long losing track of time as they sat there in front of the fire. Red had even commented it was going to start getting light in about another hour. It was just then that out of the darkness, the man who had stayed at the camp came running into the light. He was yelling he needed help, because his wife had been attacked by a bear and was hurt real bad. Red grabbed the torches that he had so carefully made and lit them from the fire, and said, " Take this torch and lead the way quickly."

The man took the torch from Red's hand and ran off into the woods with Red and Jim following close behind. When they arrived where the women was, they couldn't help but notice she had been hurt really bad and had lost a lot of blood. They knew the first thing they had to do was stop the bleeding if she was going to make it. The man from the woods just stood and watched as Red and Jim went to work to try to save her. Applying pressure to her wounds and tying off the ones that were too deep to hold, it was clear to see that she was not going to make it if she didn't get help soon. She had already lost consciousness, they just didn't know how long it had been or how much blood she had lost. In the back of their minds they couldn't help but wonder if this was the same bear they had scared away last night.

Red turned to the man and asked, "Is there any place we can take her to get help, like a hospital or a Doctor?"

The man answered, "Yes but it is too far, it would take days to get there. There is a medicine man at the far end of the lake in a cabin up into the woods.

Red and Jim both looked at each other and at the same time yelled, "The boat!"

They told the man as they carried her to the boat about how they had been lost in the fog and how when it lifted, they ended up here, it was then they asked him where they were. You could have knocked them both over with a feather when the man told them the year was eighteen hundred and one and they were on the same lake in which they had started. They knew the lake was the same but how in the world was it possible for them to go back two hundred years by passing through the fog. Right now that was not what was important, getting the woman to this medicine man was. They knew the man was not going to understand all that had happened to them and would be afraid when they started and took off in the boat. So they did their best to try to explain while they went on their way. They could tell that he was very confused but he didn't have time to be afraid now, his wife needed help anyway she could get it if she was going to live.

When they arrived at the boat it was starting to get light and the man stopped and looked at the boat as if it were some kind of evil creature that had come up from the bottom of the lake. Jim did his best to make him more comfortable by telling him it was like a canoe and there was nothing to be afraid of at all. The man still wasn't too sure he was buying all of that, but he did know his wife needed help right now and he would have to put his fear on the back burner. The three of them climbed into the boat carrying the injured woman who seemed to be getting weaker by the moment, they knew they didn't have long and she was going to die if she didn't get help. They laid her in the floor of the boat and her husband sat on the floor and placed her head on his lap as tears flowed down his face. He may have been rough and tough from living off the land, but he was still human and his emotions were still there. It was clear to see that she was all he had and he was afraid he was going to lose her. Red and Jim were determined to keep that from happening, they knew how they would feel if the shoe was on the other foot. As Red started up the boat the man's eyes seemed to scream out in fear as Jim knelt down and applied pressure to her wounds, telling him that everything was all right, just sit back and enjoy the ride. That was easy to say, but it would have been the same as Red and Jim taking off in a rocket ship bound for outer space.

As Red pulled away slowly from the shore he asked the man, "I need you to tell me where this doctor lives in the woods so we can get there fast, can you do that?"

Fisherman's Fog / 11

The man turned his head toward Red and said, "Yes, do you know the lake very well?"

Red answered, "Yes, a few things have changed but the shore line is the same."

The man replied, "It is at the far end of the lake, where two coves split off, it is in the cove to the right. Do you know where that is?"

Red shook his head and said, "Yes sir I do, now hold on this is going to be a fast ride, but everything will be just fine."

The man shook his head to let Red know he understood, but he had no idea what he was about to experience today. When Red opened up the throttle the boat jumped up on top of the water and shot across it like a bullet looking for a target. You could see the fear flowing from the man's eyes until he closed them and put his head down as if to make believe this was not really happening. Jim asked him for his name in an attempt to take his mind from his fear and he told him his name was Jake and that she was his wife and her name is Kate. In what would have taken a couple of days to travel by foot, they had made in a matter of about twenty minutes. As the boat came into the cove, the man opened his eyes to much disbelief that this was at all possible. He turned toward the shore and pointed, so Red pulled the boat to shore and the three of them lifted the woman from the boat and headed up into the woods. The man told them it was not far up into the woods where the medicine man lived and as they looked through the trees they could see the cabin with smoke coming from the chimney. That was a good sign that meant he was home and would be able to help the man and his wife. As they came walking out of the woods, they noticed a man standing at the door of the cabin. When he noticed them carrying the woman, he ran out to give them a hand.

Red asked, "Are you the doctor?"

The man looked at him and answered, "No, they call me the medicine man, because I am the closest thing they have around these parts to a doctor and always have been."

Red said, "That's good enough for me, now let's get this woman inside so you can stop the bleeding and help her out."

Once they had her inside, Red and Jim came back out to let the medicine man and her husband do what they had to do to save her. Jim couldn't help but notice that it seemed Red belonged back in this time. He seemed to be so much more at peace with himself these past few days and with his rough attitude about most things he just seemed to fit. It was as if he had been born two hundred years too late or something.

It seemed as if the two of them had sat there for hours talking about how things had changed so much through those years, when the door of the cabin came open and out walked the medicine man. He walked over to Jim and Red and extended his hand and said, "Thanks to you two gentlemen, the woman looks like she is going to make it, as long as infection doesn't set in."

Jim answered, "That's great, we were glad we could help."

The medicine man said, "My name is William and I heard you coming a long way off, because the sounds carry so well across the water. It has been a long time since I heard a sound like that and I knew what it was before you ever got here."

Jim asked, "How is that possible."

William answered with a smile on his face, "I came through the fog about twenty years ago, just like you have."

Red looked at Jim and then back to William and asked, "Are you telling me that you came through the fog twenty years ago and that you are still stuck here?"

William smiled once again and said, "No, not stuck here, I choose to remain here. I believe I could have left anytime I chose by simply going back out into the fog when it is there."

Jim couldn't help but ask, "Where are you from and why do you stay if you could leave through the fog?"

William answered, "I am from Southern Illinois and was a Doctor in a small community and was never married. I always came up here to the lake alone for two weeks every year, just to get away so no one could bother me. You know how it is, if you don't get away they will not leave you alone. After I passed through the fog, I decided to stay. I always believed that I could get back through the fog if I chose to do so, just never chose to."

Jim replied, "Well if nothing else here makes sense at least that does, and that also explains the medicine man thing as well."

William said, "Yes, it lets me still help those who need help, but also lets me live a life that I enjoy very much."

This made sense to Jim and Red because they had both said just the other night how much more they loved it here now than before coming through the fog. Then Jim asked, "How do you know when the time is right to go back through the fog, because it is foggy almost every morning this time of year?"

William said, "You will know the fog is right because you will hear nothing, not a bird sing, or a cricket chirp, everything will become calm and not a sound will be heard. Sometimes it doesn't happen for years and then again I have seen it only a few days apart, you just never know when."

After thinking about it, they knew what he was saying was right because they noticed how quiet it was while they were out there that foggy morning. They were very happy to know this, because now they knew when the time was right, they would be able to return home. They both decided right then and there they would try to go home the next time they noticed such a fog in the air.

Red asked, "Doc, how do you know that by going back into the fog you will get back, have you tried it yet.

William smiled a little and answered, "Well, you got me there friend, no I have not, but it was the only thing that made any sense to me when I tried to figure out how this could happen. Through these years I have been tempted several times to venture out into that fog, but was never willing to take the chance of not being able to get back here again."

William put them up at the cabin for the next several weeks until Kate was well enough to travel and he was very happy to do so. Because it gave him a chance to catch up on things he had missed, after all Red and Jim were from Southern Illinois as well and he knew a lot of the places they talked about. Red had asked him if he missed being home and he had replied that this was more home for him than he had ever had before. Red knew exactly what he meant because he loved the unchanged surroundings here and felt very much at peace. He had often said in the past several weeks how he felt closer to the Lord here. William seemed to think that he was guided here by the Lord to help the people from here, who had no one else to turn to and he was very grateful for that. He also told them he believed the Lord had brought them here that one foggy day so they would be here to save the life of the woman attacked by the bear. Because if they had not been there, she would have died for sure. Jake just sat and listened to all of the things that were being said and you could tell that it was all beginning to make sense to him finally.

Jake stood up and said, "Then you are all angels of the Lord sent from heaven?"

Red said, "No, not angels, just servants I guess you could say. We are all guided down a path in life so we can

Fisherman's Fog / 15

be where we are meant to be, to do the things the Lord has for us to do. We were just sent a little farther this time I guess.

You could tell that Jake really didn't understand all of this, but one thing he did know was he was very happy that they came along when they did. At first when they scared him away from his camp he was sorry to see them arrive, but now he knew he was very pleased to have met them both.

The day finally came when Kate was well enough to travel back to the camp where they had been living, so they all returned to the boat. They shook hands with William and thanked him for everything and Jake told him that he would try to drop by when Kate was better and drop off some deer meat for him as payment for all he had done. William told him it was not necessary but Jake wouldn't take no for an answer and William just nodded his head and told him thanks.

Red turned to William and shook his hand and asked, "Well Doc, when we return home through the fog is there anything you would like us to do for you?"

William smiled and answered, " No thanks Red, even if anyone remembered me, they would never believe you if you told them. I left that life behind and to me it doesn't exist anymore, this is my life now, but have a safe trip."

Jim shook his hand as well and told him good-bye and thanked him for everything as well. Then they slipped away from the shore in a very light fog and down the lake. He stood and watched them disappear around the edge of the cove, but he could still hear the purr of the engine as they shot across the lake. He stood there for a while thinking about everything that had happened these past few weeks. As he stood there listening the fog began to thicken and the sounds began to fade, he knew what all of this would mean to Red, Jim, Jake and Kate if they had not made their way across the lake yet, if they had finally made it back to the camp they would be fine.

The problem was they had not made it back to the camp and they were now trapped out in the fog once again. They sat there in the fog as it muffled out all sound and light. Red and Jim knew what this meant and they knew this was a problem, not for the two of them, but it would be for Jake and Kate. Jim started explaining to the two of them about the fog they came through before and that the Doctor believed the fog would send them back. Then he explained to them both that they would probably be returning to a time two hundred years in the future for them. This was a little frightening for both of them but they realized there wasn't a lot they could do about it now. They all sat quietly listening for any sign of movement or sound and there was nothing, it was perfectly calm. Then two and a half hours later the fog began to clear, just like before and they could see the shore line littered with cabins and houses that were not there before they had entered the fog. Red turned the boat toward where they had been staying before they entered the fog the first time and sure enough their cabin was there. He pulled the boat to shore and as he stepped out to the shore the owner of the cabin was walking down to meet them with a puzzled look on his face.

The owner said, "Where the Sam hell have you two guys been? They had a search party looking for you guys for about a week and then they gave up all hope of finding you. You have been gone for about a month now.

Jim tried his best to explain to him what had happened, but he wasn't buying any about this story and told them he was glad to see they were all right and that was good enough for him. He told them he had put all of their belongings up at his place and they could pick them up on their way out, because the cabins had all been closed up for the winter. Jim went up to the house and called his family and told them that he was fine and that he would explain everything when he got home. They were very happy to hear from him and they had said they had never given up hope that he was all right and would return in time. Red and Jim were known for getting a little to involved with what they were doing and losing track of time, just never this long before, normally a couple of days or maybe a week, but not for a month. Red lived alone so this was never a problem for him, he just returned home whenever he pleased and had no one to answer to, just the way he liked it.

The problem now was what to do about Jake and Kate, the boat was frightening enough to the both of them. Now they were going to have to get them into a car and try to get them home without scaring them both to death. They all talked it over and since Red was living alone in a house out in a wooded area, he would take them back to his place and try to help them adjust to all the changes that they would have to encounter. After all no one knew when the fog would return, it could be years or maybe even never, then what were the odds of them ever being on the lake at the right time again.

They pulled the boat from the water while Jake and Kate sat petrified in the back seat of Red's old station wagon. Then down the road they went slow but surely, trying to give the two of them a chance to adjust a little. Kate began to cry a bit and Jake kept telling her everything was going to be all right, then he would look at Jim to convince himself and Jim would smile and give him a nod signaling he was right. After ten hours of driving to get back to Reds, Jake and Kate were amazed at all the things they had seen along the way, each being a miracle in their minds and confusing just the same. Everything seemed to move so fast to them it was frightening. It was as if life was flying by, Jake had commented as Kate sat quietly with the look of fear in her eyes. When they arrived at Red's home, there was an opening where his driveway turned in through the trees and back into his little piece of heaven. No neighbors or traffic, a little more like the world they had just come from except he lived in a house instead of the shelters that had been built there.

Red welcomed them into his home and Jim helped unload all of the gear and help them get settled in and then he told Red that he would check in on him later. He knew he needed to get home to his family and try to explain all of this to them as well. Red knew they were waiting for him and told him to go on and that everything was going to be all right for now and they would figure out what to do about Jake and Kate later, after everything settled down just a bit. Jim jumped into his truck and down the driveway and through the woods he disappeared.

When he arrived home the family was all waiting for him and very happy to see him again, his wife made a few remarks about him being gone so long, but she was happy to see him just the same. He started right away telling them all about everything that had happened and he could tell by the time he was done, they weren't too sure they were buying this little story. So he told them tomorrow he was taking them all over to Red's to met Jake and Kate and after they saw them they would know he was telling them all the truth. Jim was tired from the long trip and they all decided to call it a night and just be grateful that they were all back together again.

The next morning bright and early they all loaded up into his family car and drove back over to Red's to meet the mystery couple. It was clear to them all after talking to the two of them the story they had been told was very true. Jake and Kate were a little overwhelmed by all of the new faces and Jim told his family that it was time to go and told Red he would come back over in about a week to see how they were all doing. Red agreed that he thought the time alone would be a good thing for Jake and Kate.

For a couple of days Red was very patient with both of them trying to help them adjust to the changes in life, but he could tell they were not happy, He felt bad that he had brought them back, but he also knew that he had no control over that at all. Just like he had told Jake before, he explained to him again, about the Lord putting us where we are meant to be when we are meant to be there. Jake seemed to understand and commented how the Lord had brought Red and Jim through the fog to save his wife and he was very grateful for that, but he wasn't too sure what the Lord had in mind for him when He brought them back here. Red didn't have the answer for that either and knew the only thing they could do was to wait and see.

At the end of the week Jim returned to Red's to find the station wagon and the boat both gone and no one at home.

The door was unlocked and he was concerned maybe something had happened, so he opened the door and yelled inside asking if anyone was home, but no one answered. He looked over to the kitchen table and noticed a note laying there with his name on the outside. He opened it slowly almost knowing what it was going to say.

The note read,

> "Jim, I have taken Jake and Kate back to the lake and we are going to go out everyday until the fog returns. They both told me they wanted to go back home more than anything else in life, I feel as if they deserve that. I believe they were brought back here to see what life will become, so they can help others with what they have learnt."
>
> P.S. "I don't know if I will return, God willing I will see you again my friend. I will say Hi to the Doc for you."
>
> RED

It has been one year since Red left and he has still to this day not been heard from. Jim returned to the lake several times throughout the past year and has yet to see such a fog again. But he knows that someday either himself or Red will stumble across that magical fog again and will be reunited. Until then he knows Red will be very happy living where he has gone.

The Search

It has been six long years since the day Red disappeared into the fog and Jim has returned up to the lake several times each year trying to search for him. Although he found the fog to be thick many times, he never found the special place that would send him back to his old friend and his new home. He has told many people about his adventure and no one believed him, except for his family that had met Jake and Kate. After they had met them there was no way they could have denied what had truly happened. He has missed his old friend and had hoped, if just for a while, he could have seen him again. He knew how much more Red loved the life there and was not at all surprised when he had found a way to return and take Jake and Kate with him. Now the question would be, would he ever see his old friend again?

The next year Jim returned to the lake once again in the spring, just after the ice had all melted from the water. The second day after he had arrived he noticed a fog sat in on the lake, so he grabbed his things and into his boat he hurried. Slowly he motored out onto the lake, careful not to run into anything else that may have been out on the lake that day. He sat out in the fog for several hours, but when it finally lifted he was still right where he had started, the date had never changed. He stayed at the lake for two full weeks hoping for his chance to return back in time to his old friend, but it was not meant to be. He returned home wondering if he would indeed ever see his old friend Red again and if he was all right.

A thought had popped into Jim's mind about whether any of Red's family was still living or if they were wondering what had happened to him since he had vanished. So he set out on a mission to search for his family, to see if he was able to find them. He returned to the old house where Red had lived and it was still just like he had left it. He had been by the place about two years ago and found a note tacked to the front door, it read, "Notice of delinquent taxes." He went to the county courthouse and paid the taxes due on the property and has kept them paid ever since. As he arrived to the house this time, he went inside to check to see if there would have been any kind of mail or paper work that would give him a clue to where he might find a living relative. Back in the corner of one of the closets he found a box of old Christmas cards Red had been saving. They must have meant something to him because they looked very old and he wasn't even sure all the people who had sent them were even still alive. As he thumbed through the box he found one that was signed, Love Mom. The card was still in the original envelope and the address was a little faded but he was able to make it out. At least this was a start, now all he had to do was hope this woman was still alive and living in the same location. After all, Red was now fifty-six years old and that would have made her at least seventy-five or six, the way he figured.

The address on the envelope was up in Wisconsin, so Jim drove all night to get there. When he arrived, he walked up to the door and knocked and there was no answer, so he knocked again and waited patiently, hoping for someone to come. Then, about the time he was going to turn and walk away, the door slowly started to open and there stood an old woman that looked as if she was very old, much older than he was expecting.

She opened the door and asked, "Hello, may I help you with something?"

Jim answered, "Yes, I was hoping you could help me. I am looking for a Mrs. Benny."

She smiled and said, "Then you are in luck young man, because you have found her."

She asked him to come inside and he was a little surprised that she had, because now days it seemed no one trusted anyone they did not know. She didn't seem to be bothered by any of that as if she had not been exposed to all of the corruption in the world, and that was nice to see. She walked him into the living room and asked him to have a seat and he thanked her very much. She then sat down and asked him what this was all about and how it had anything to do with her.

Unsure how to start the conversation, he asked, "I need to know a few things and I thought maybe you could help."

She answered, "I am an old woman and my mind is not what it used to be, but I will be happy to answer your questions if I can."

Jim replied, "Do you have a son that is known as Red?"

With a very worried look on her face she answered, "Yes I do, has something happened to my son?"

Jim smiled and said, "No, I am sorry if I alarmed you. He is a very good friend of mine and I am looking for him and thought maybe you had heard from him."

She answered, "No, I haven't heard from him for about six years now and am very worried about where he might be and if he is alright."

It was then he told her about the day he and Red had experienced the fog, and where it had taken them and that they had returned home. Then how he found a note on his table telling him Red had gone back to that place in the fog and it was the last time he had seen him.

She smiled and said, "Well, I think I might be able to shed some light on this little story, but it may take some time, would you care to have a cup of tea with me while I tell you a little story?"

Not sure what she could be talking about he answered, "Yes that would be very nice, thank you."

When she got up to go to the kitchen, thoughts raced through his mind of what news she could possibly have to share with him that he wouldn't already know about this situation. He had barely touched base on the subject of the two of them going off into the fog, but it was as if she believed every word he had said. This was something no one wanted to believe, so why was it so easy for her to accept?

When she returned with the tea, she sat it down on the table and slowly sat back down in her chair. She looked at Jim and asked him if he wanted to hear about a family secret that had been passed down through the family from her mother, about her Great Grandmother. He told her he would be honored to hear anything she was willing to share with him and how she reminded him of her son when he looked into her eyes. This brought a smile to her face as she reached over and began to pour the tea into the two cups sitting on the table. She then started telling him about a story that her mother had told her about her Great Grandmother and how she had lived in the wilderness up in northern Wisconsin. How she had told a story about how she and her husband had lived off the land in the wild and how she had been attacked by a bear and two strange gentlemen from another world, far into the future, had came to save her life. She claimed one of the men had hair the color of fire and the other hair the color of the sandy soil. Then how they traveled in machines that were faster than the wind could blow, carrying her to the doctor for help. Jim sat quietly with a smile on his face and continued to listen, amazed at the details of the story that had not been changed in all of these years and how what he had experienced had come to life in the minds of so many generations of people. They both sat quietly for a moment sipping their tea, as Jim thought carefully about what to say next.

After sitting for a spell, he started telling her his version of the story about how they had sat out in the fog that damp morning for two and a half hours to find themselves in another time when the fog had lifted. He told her how they had scared the two people away and how the man had come to them for help after his wife had been attacked by the bear and they had taken her to the medicine man. As he told the story he could see her face light up with joy, just knowing that it was her son who had saved her distant relative. Jim continued by telling her that they had returned home with the two people that they had found and how they were not happy here and how her son Red had taken them back through the fog. He told her that he had went back each and every year trying to find his way back through the fog but had never found it again.

She smiled at me and said, "My mother told me once that there was another way to this place."

Jim sat there with his mouth hanging open looking like a fool and just had to ask, "I am dying to know the answer to this secret, if you will please tell me."

She answered, "I would be happy to tell you if I could remember, but it was when I was a small child, all I remember it was in a hidden passageway under ground. It was a Federal building that had been built over it somewhere on the East Coast, to conceal the location. The rooms were said to be made of cobble stone, walls and floors, with different doors leading from place to place. When you would step on a certain stone the room would spin and when it would stop, you would be in a different time and place. My Mother told of a long hallway with several doors to pass through and through the last doorway was the way back to her time and place. The opening behind the door was a cavern of some sort."

Jim sat with a blank stare on his face not knowing what to say next, wondering where this place could be and what the possibilities of ever finding it may be. It was then that he asked her how she knew of this place. She began telling him of how her mother's Great Grandmother was having a baby and because of the damage the bear had caused her she was not going to survive. The man with the hair of fire took her back to the medicine man and they decided she was not going to make it without more help than he could give her. It was then the medicine man told the man with red hair about the door that he hid under a bear skin rug on his floor. He had built his cabin over the hole in the ground that leads to the cavern of time. They had decided that the only way she and the baby were going to survive was to take them through the cavern, into the cobble stone rooms and out for help, and then return when they were ready to travel.

Jim was having a hard time believing his own ears at everything Mrs. Benny was telling him, even though he had been through some of this himself. He knew of no such cavern, or cobble stone rooms, or hallways that lead through time. He couldn't help but ask her if she knew the names of the man and the woman who would have been her Great, Great Grandparents.

She smiled and looked him right in the eyes and said, "Yes, their names were Jake and Kate. I never met them but I remember my mother's stories very well and that they were always a family secret."

He knew then and there she was telling the truth, because he had never told her their names. It was all starting to make sense to him now, the baby had to be Mrs. Benny's own Great Grandmother. But before he could say another word, there was a knock at the door.

Mrs. Benny had a strange look on her face and replied about how she had gone months without anyone knocking on her door and now it had happened twice in one day. Jim found this to be a little strange as well, if this were true, but when she opened the door you could have knocked him over with a feather. There stood Red with his hair long and pulled back into a pony tail and some kind of fur cap on his head. He reached down and gave his mother a hug and told her he had missed her and then walked over and hugged Jim as well. He told him that he wished he had gone back with him, but he knew he had a family here and knew it would not be fair to ask such a thing.

Jim couldn't help but ask, "Red, what are you doing here and why have you returned?"

He answered, "It is Kate, she is having a baby and the Doc, believe it or not, had a hidden passageway in his floor to get back here. Imagine that, he had the chance to tell us that before and never said a thing."

Jim looked at Red and said, "You better sit down my friend, because you are never going to believe what your mother has just informed me of."

Jim told Red about the stories that his mother had told about the two men and that this was passed on from her Great, Great Grandmother. He sat there for a few moments and then he could tell by the look on Red's face that he understood this would mean that Kate was his Great, Great, Great grandmother. His face lit up like a campfire and a smile filled his face, for the first time since he had passed through the fog, he now understood this all had a purpose. In some strange way he had played a part in his own existence, with the birth of this child and the rescue of Kate from the bear attack.

He burst out laughing and said, "Remember how we scared them away when we arrived that day from the fog? Well, I should have figured it out then and there, my family has always thought I was a little strange, but they were the first to run from me."

Jim laughed right along with him as he pictured Jake running from them that day. It was then he asked Red how he entered back into this time and place from the hole in Doc's floor. He told Jim that when they came to the end of the cavern there was a wooden door that had been jammed from being closed for so many years. After several attempts of throwing his shoulder into it, he was able to bust it open, placing them here in a hallway of cobblestone walls and floors that looked very old. After going through several more rooms and doors they found a stone stairway up to the house and pushed the door open that had been hidden behind the wall. He mentioned a man named Norman whom he scared the crap out of, and a very kind woman named Sara, they were now living in this home. They helped get Kate to the hospital as soon as possible, because they could see she was in need of help and fast. They tried to answer all of their questions on the way to the hospital.

Red told Jim and his Mother that Kate and the baby were doing fine, they told the hospital she was a homeless woman with no records of any kind, to avoid answering many questions they would never believe anyway. He said that he would be leaving to go back in a couple of days and that he wanted to see them before he returned. Jim asked him how he was going to return and he told him through the cobblestone room. He stated that Norman and Sara told them their secret was safe with them and they would be happy to help them when it was time to return home. Red commented on how wonderful and helpful these two people really were to them and he would remember that forever.

Red turned to his mother and asked, "Mom, would you like to go meet Kate and the baby?"

She answered, "Yes with all of my heart, but I am too old to travel that far."

Jim stood up and said, "You are never too old to have a chance like this. Come on, I will drive, my car is right outside and ready to go."

Mom ran to gather a few things and Red said, "Thanks Jim, it took me two days to get here and we figured it would take me two days to get back. Then it would be time for us all to head back through the cavern and back home."

They drove all night and in the morning they arrived at the hospital and Red's mother went into the room to see Kate just before she and the baby were going to be released. Mrs. Benny sat and held the baby in her arms and tears rolled down her face as Kate sat with a smile on her face, because Red had just broken the news to her who this woman really was. Then he told her she was his mother, this brought tears to Kate's eyes as well to know that he had been the one who had come back in time to save her for the second time.

After leaving the hospital they returned to the home of Norman and Sara, where the Doc had been kindly allowed to stay. While he was there, he thought it was only fair to fill them in on everything that had happened up to this point and how important it was for them to keep it to themselves. They understood how this would change everything and agreed to keep the secret and to lock those doors behind them as they left. Kate handed the baby to Sara and told her that she was grateful for everything they had done to help them and wished she could do something to repay them. Sara told her that was not necessary, they were just honored to have been a part of everything and thankful they shared this with them. Sara looked down at the baby and then looked over to Norman with a sparkle in her eyes and Norman just shook his head as to say no. Something about holding a baby makes women miss not having one of their own at times, and Norman wasn't about to let those ideas get started again. So she gently kissed the baby on the forehead and handed her back to Kate.

Now it was time to leave. Kate, Jake, Doc and Red all walked through the stone stairs and as Red went to pull it closed behind him he reached out and hugged his mother and told her that Jim would see her home safely. Then he turned to Jim and shook his hand and said, "I will see you soon, my friend, I will see you soon." He then pulled the wall panel closed behind him.

Jim thanked Norman and Sara for everything, as he told them to watch out for which stone on the floor they step on down there. Because the trick was not leaving, the trick is finding the way back. He had found that out the hard way. They both told Jim that they would watch their step. Mrs. Benny and Jim climbed back into the car and drove away as this old woman waved out the window like she was a young girl again. Jim believed this one thing had truly given her the will to live on and something to fill her heart.

Jim drove all that day to get her back home and made sure everything was all right before he left. As he was leaving she grabbed a hold of him and pulled him in and gave him the hug of his life. She gently kissed him on the cheek and told him how grateful she was to him for knocking on her door that wonderful day. He thanked her as well and walked away waving as he climbed into the car and drove away.

Jim felt so much better now and understood everything that had happened was for a reason. Many people's lives would have been so much different if they had not gone out into the fog that late fall day. He looks forward to seeing his friend Red again. Just hearing him say that he would see him again soon, was enough to fill him full of hope. Now every time he hears a knock at the door, he knows it could be his friend. When Jim sits out on the lake and the fog moves in, he closes his eyes and thinks of it as the gentle kiss of the Lord as it touches his face.

The Stone

It has been over a year since Red, Jake, Kate and the baby had traveled down the cobble stone hallway at the home of Norman and Sara. It is snowing outside and there is more snow on the ground than many people had seen in these parts for many, many years. It is very late and earlier Norman had turned all the lights on outside the house so he could sit by the window and watch as the snow fell so peacefully from the sky. As he sat there, memories of what had happened over a year ago raced through his mind. He was amazed that he and Sara were able to keep the secret of the passageway from everyone. A smile came across his face as he remembered Sara standing there that special day, holding Kate's baby, and how special that moment was to both of them. Soon he grew tired and ventured upstairs to join his lovely wife and slip off to a peaceful night of sleep.

Sometime during the night, Sara's brother Robert entered the home, bringing with him a large black raven by the name of Rex. He carried Rex in his cage as he walked into the den, careful to not make any noise and wake everyone up in the house. Rex had been injured years ago and was unable to fly, so he had become a pet and part of the family to everyone. Rex had started a little bit of a commotion at Robert's home, so he thought it best if he brought him over to Norman and Sara's for the night, just to let things settle down a bit. It was very peaceful here and he thought it would give Rex a chance to settle down as well. Robert sat the cage down in the den and closed the door, with plans to come back in the morning to retrieve Rex and his cage. Just as quietly as he had entered, Robert left the house and locked up behind himself, with Norman and Sara never even knowing he had been there that night.

Shortly after Robert had left the home, Norman was having a hard time falling to sleep, so he decided to go downstairs and drink a warm glass of soy milk to help him sleep. As he slipped on his robe, Sara sat up and asked him where he was going with a startled look in her eyes. Norman told her that everything was all right, that he was just going downstairs for a glass of warm milk. She told him to wait, that she would go with him because it sounded good to her as well. After they had made their way down the stairs and almost into the kitchen, they heard a horrible noise coming from the den. The doors were shut and the lights were off and it scared the hell out of both of them, as they both stood there motionless.

Sara had such a death grip on Norman's robe he couldn't get away even if he had tried. He walked her into the kitchen and then went in to see what it could have been that was making the noise. Before he could open the door, he heard it again, followed by a horrible scratching, tearing sound. Norman found himself completely petrified of thoughts that somehow something had made its way up from the passageway and was now behind those doors. As he slid the door open slowly and managed to hit the lights, there stood Rex, ripping papers and making quite the mess of things. He had somehow managed to get out of his cage and was having his way with everything in the room. The thing was Norman had no idea how Rex had gotten there and called for Sara to come and see the surprise that he had discovered. Sara knew then and there that Robert must have slipped in during the night and left Rex. Norman and Sara directed Rex carefully back to his cage and closed his gate and then called Robert on the phone to ask him what was going on. He explained to them why he had dropped Rex off, that he was sorry for the mess and he would be over in the morning to pick him up, bright and early.

The next morning, bright and early as he had promised, Robert was there to pick up Rex and his mess. When he arrived he noticed that Norman and Sara must have left early that morning. They would run to the docks to pick up fresh produce and seafood from time to time. As he walked into the den he noticed that Rex had once again escaped his large cage and was once again wandering throughout the house somewhere. As Robert searched the house he came around the corner, and there stood Rex at the other end of the long hallway, staring a hole right through Robert with those deep dark eyes that Ravens have. This sent a chill down Robert's spine as he walked slowly toward Rex with hopes that he would not attack him. About the time Robert reached the halfway point of the hallway, Rex reached over and started to pull at a piece of molding along the wall. Robert thought to himself, "That's all I need now is for that darn bird to start tearing up the wall trim," so he would have to fix that too. He yelled at Rex to stop as he continued to tear away at the wall trim with a vengeance. As Robert came closer, he noticed that it was a line or a break in the trim along the wall, so he reached into the little hole that Rex had created and gave the wall a little pull. When he pulled, the wall began to open and behind this wall was a large solid wooden door. Robert, always being the curious type, couldn't help but see what surprises might lay behind this door. He thought to himself, "What the heck, it can't hurt to at least open the door and take a peek in to see what might be there." As he forced the old wooden door open, Rex went running through into the darkness, and Robert thought to himself once again, "That damn bird is always getting me into something or making a mess for me to clean up." He knew it would do no good to call for Rex because he was not like a dog at all, he would not come when you called for him. He would only come when he wanted to attack something or try to scare something away. Robert couldn't see much from where he was standing, other than there was an old stone stairway that seem to wind its way down to a lower level of some sort. He left the door open and ran to the kitchen to get the flashlight that he knew was always kept there in case of an emergency.

When Robert returned to the passageway he stood there with the flashlight shining down the stone stairway, curious but a little concerned. He called for Rex even though he knew that was a waste of his time. As he stood there listening for any sounds that Rex may have been making, he heard nothing. As he worked his way down the stairway he couldn't believe what he was seeing, all the walls and floors were of cobblestone. Then he noticed over in the far corner of the room stood Rex, with a strange look in his eye like he had a little secret of his own that he had discovered or something.

As Robert panned the flashlight around the room he noticed another doorway that looked as if it lead to another room, but he was not about to adventure any further for now, all he wanted was to get Rex and get out of here. As he walked carefully across the cobblestones he kept the flashlight on Rex, just in case he decided to make a run for it again. He was hoping that by keeping the light in his eyes he would not move because he could not see, but just as he reached for Rex, he placed his foot on a stone and felt it begin to move. In fact the whole room seemed to begin to move in a circular motion that was very slow at first as he looked down at Rex, but then started to spin at a much higher rate, until it was spinning so fast he found himself completely disoriented.

When the room finally came to rest, Robert couldn't believe his eyes, he was standing in a trench or ditch about four feet deep and could hear gunfire everywhere around him. He noticed two other men lying in the trench near by and they were both wearing uniforms of the union army from back in the civil war. He sat down in the trench and tried to make some kind of sense from all of this, but couldn't believe all that was happening and so fast. He knew right then and there that if he was to be caught by the army, they would shoot him thinking he was either fighting for the other side or a spy of some sort. So he gently, but quickly removed one of the uniforms from the men lying there in the trench. He figured they weren't going to need them any more and it may very well save his life. He also grabbed a rifle and the ammunition belt from one of the men. The only concern that he had at this point was that he had chosen the right uniform for the battle if he was to survive.

After Robert got himself dressed, he worked his way across what seemed to be a large cemetery of some sort. As gunfire rang out he dove into another trench and found himself with another young boy, who was sitting down in the hole clenching his rifle with both hands, so tight he could see that his knuckles were turning white. As Robert hunched down in the trench, he looked at the young boy and said, "Son, I seemed to have hit my head and I am not sure where I am right now. Can you help me out?"

The young boy turned his head and looked at Robert and said, "Sure can mister, you are in a fight for your life and country, this is the Battle of Gettysburg and this is Cemetery Ridge."

Robert knew from history that this was not a good thing at all, he remembered this was a battle that lasted three days, and the Union troops had won this battle. At least he had put on the right uniform if his odds of surviving were going to be their best. He remembered that it was a fierce battle between both sides and how this had been the turning point of the war and that the South, led by Robert E. Lee, had lost more than twenty five thousand men. The reason that this was a turning point in the war was because never again would Lee have the troop support to launch another major offensive.

Robert turned to the young boy and asked, "How many days have we been fighting here?

The young boy, with the look of fear deeply planted in his eyes, answered, "Today is the third day, and in the last two days I have lost my brother and all of my friends from back home."

Robert moved over to the young boy and told him, "I am sorry about your brother and your friends, but trust me it will all be over soon."

The boy turned to Robert and said, "Mister how the hell do you know that, you can't even remember where the hell you are."

Robert looked down to the ground to gather his thoughts and then looked back up to the young boy and answered, "Because I have enough faith for the both of us."

As Robert sat there in the trench, thoughts came to mind of what would happen if it even came to the point where he would be forced to fire his weapon on another living soul. He wondered if it change history forever, since he was not supposed to even be here at all. It was then and there that he decided that he was just going to sit and ride out the battle and only fire his weapon if it was necessary to save his or the young boy in the trenches lives. As he sat there in the trench with bullets flying overhead, he couldn't help but think to himself, "Look what that damn bird has gotten me into again." He thought Rex must not have made the trip, he must have come alone since he was the one who stepped upon the stone. But for some reason he couldn't help but think that somehow Rex knew about that stone, by the way he was standing there tempting him to come toward him.

Just then things became very quiet, the firing had stopped and for a few moments things seemed to be at peace. Then all hell broke loose. The final attack of the battle of Gettysburg had begun. Robert heard screaming of the men on the move, as thirteen thousand Confederate troops came marching toward them in perfect parade formation, as they came sweeping across the fields and up the slopes of Cemetery Ridge. The battle was fierce and long as the gunfire rang out and cannon fire blasted the fields of the approaching troops. Robert couldn't help himself as he pulled himself up from the floor of the trench and watched as history unfolded right there before him. He had thoughts of how sad it was for so many young and old men to die on this and every day of this war, because he knew that in many ways it was not what it would take to change things in the future. He knew how that battle would not end here on these battlefields with the death of all of these brave men. It would be pushed on into the courtrooms and halls of justice to still never be resolved in the hearts of all men, women and children. He knew this would only be resolved in the heart and souls of everyone who knew the difference between what is morally right in the eyes of the Lord and that indeed all men were created equal. The sad thing was to him that even though all of these men would die as so many have already, one hundred-fifty years later this battle would still be fought by some and generations would pass down their prejudices to one another standing in the way of freedom for all.

In the midst of all the battle, it was the first time he had seen things this clearly, something you can not understand by reading a book or sitting in a classroom listening to a teacher who had never been there at all. History has a strange way of changing in the eyes of all of those who look back on it, but for the first time in Robert's life, he was seeing it first hand, unfolding right before his eyes. He watched with heartache as so many young men fell as they crossed the field that morning, all of them being shot down or captured if they reached Cemetery Ridge.

After a long day of standing their ground, Robert watched with shock in his eyes, as a single Confederate soldier made his way toward the trench where he and the young boy had been watching. Robert felt the fear of battle racing through his heart as it began to beat faster and faster. "What am I to do?" he thought, "Should I fire on him or not?" Those were the thoughts that jumbled his mind. Then before he knew what to do next the soldier was standing before him and the young boy, as he heard two shots ring out. Robert knew he had not fired a shot but it was then that he realized that the young boy in the trench with him had shot and killed the Confederate solder who had looked down upon them. It was also then that Robert realized the first shot of the two had struck him in the chest, seeming to pierce the same exact hole in the jacket that had killed the original soldier who had worn the jacket earlier. Confusion raced through his mind, wondering if this was the end for him and if his family and friends would even know what had become of him. This entire thing, he thought, because of that damn Raven and the messes he gets me into.

As the young soldier pressed down hard on his wound and told him to hold on, Robert's eyes began to close, as he felt himself slowly slipping away. In a matter of moments, Robert found himself very much at peace and could not hear the gunfire ringing out overhead any longer. Then just as he had entered this place and time, the world around him began to spin faster and faster as the moments passed. Then all of a sudden, Robert felt a hard thud against his back and found he was awake and lying on the cobble stone floor of the home of Norman and Sara once again. He was wearing the uniform of the Union soldier and the hole from the bullet was still there, but he found himself not wounded at all.

Very confused about what had just happened, he picked himself up and carefully moved toward the stone stairway which he could barely see due to the light shining down from the door being left open upstairs, where he had entered.

As he stepped into the hallway and closed the passageway behind himself, he turned to see Norman and Sara standing, looking at him with amazement. They had come home to find Rex running freely throughout the house, leaving his friendly little deposits behind. They had also noticed that someone had left the passageway door open, but they were unsure about whom. Their first thought was that maybe Red had returned, as he had promised his mother, or maybe Jim had become tired of waiting for him to return and had ventured out on his own to find his friend. The last thing they were expecting was for dear old Robert to come popping out of the door wearing a uniform of the Union army.

Robert began telling them about his adventure and that he had found the passageway thanks to Rex, then how he had stepped on the stone and things began to spin, finding him in a different place and time. He stopped and thought about all that he was saying and said, "I know this all sounds really crazy and it is hard for you to believe, but it is all true."

Norman and Sara looked at each other and smiled as Norman replied, "We do indeed believe you Robert, we have known about the room for some time now."

Robert sat there with a shocked look on his face, looking down then back up to Norman and said, "What the hell do you mean you knew it was there for some time now, why didn't you tell me?"

Sara answered, "Because we promised the person who had shown us the passageway that we would not tell anyone."

Robert started to laugh and said, "That is one crazy room you have down there. Please watch where you step, you never know where you may end up."

Norman replied, "Yes, we know, that is why we never go down there and you must tell no one about this room."

Robert replied, "You have my word on that one, but I don't understand how I got back here. I know I stepped on the stone and it sent me there but how did I get back?"

Sara remembered something that they had been told and said, "We were told that the trick wasn't getting somewhere, the trick would be how to get back."

Robert smiled and answered, "Well, I think I found the way back from this one, it was death. I had been shot and I guess since I had never lived in that time before, I could not die there either."

This all made sense to Norman and Sara. After all, they had already seen things most people would have never believed that came from the room down below. Robert pulled the jacket from his chest in an effort to show them where the bullet had entered. Even though the hole remained in the jacket, there was no sign or mark on Robert at all. Robert told them both someday he would like to go down in the room again and check things out but it would be in the distant future, because he had seen and experienced all he could handle for a very long time. He told them all about the battle and what he had seen first hand, then about the young boy who had tried to save his life. He couldn't help but wonder what had happened to the young boy as the day went on, he hoped that he had lived on to keep the family name alive, since he had known he lost his brother. Norman and Sara sat with amazement and listened to everything Robert had to tell, and when he had finished, they all hugged one another realizing how lucky they all were to still be together.

Norman sat and told Robert all about Red, Jake and Kate and how they had come out from the passageway on that special day the baby was to arrive. Robert understood now why they had kept their promise to keep the passageway a secret. Norman reminded Robert that he must tell no one of the passageway and Robert agreed it would be best if no one ever knew. Then, as he peeled off his dirty old uniform, Robert began mumbling something about wondering where the heck that big black bird had run off to now. Norman and Sara just sat at the table and laughed as Robert ran about the house in what looked like a pair of old long-johns and socks, searching for old Rex.

The Judgment

Many months had passed since Robert returned from deep within the cobblestone room, and not a sound or whisper about the room had been spoken. The rooms below remained sealed and no one had ventured down or up those stone steps since he had returned. The snow was now falling so softly out on the lawn and was starting to build, blanketing everything in sight. Sara stood at the window and watched, as Mother Nature seemed to change the world around her. She stood at the tall windows and watched patiently, waiting for Norman to return from a trip he had taken to the West Coast. It was rare for Norman to make those trips alone and she missed him so much while he was away. She had kept Rex for a couple of days as a favor to Robert, figuring he might keep her company as well while Norman was away. The problem was Rex never seemed to stay where he was supposed to be, every time she would go to check on him in his cage, he had somehow managed to escape.

Sara sat down on the window ledge and opened a book she had started reading a few days before. From time to time she would raise her head and look back out upon the snow, to see how much more had fallen. She was very concerned about Norman traveling through the snow and was hoping he would not be delayed in his return to her this evening. She had waited all week for him to return and didn't want anything to stand in the way of their reunion. She saw a small black bird fly past the window and it reminded her of Rex and instantly she thought she had better check on him because he had not made a sound for hours and that was unlike him. He was usually tearing into something or letting out a screech just to get someone's attention and he had become quite the master at picking his lock and opening the door to his cage. As she walked into the den, she noticed once again he had pulled the Houdini act of escape and was wandering freely around the house. Sara picked up a newspaper to defend herself, just in case Rex decided to surprise her as she ventured around a corner and attack her. He was known for doing those things. He had caught Robert off guard several times, so she was going to be prepared.

She wandered from room to room without a sign of Rex anywhere, and last but not least she entered the long hallway that lead to the passageway. When she peeked around the corner, like a young child playing hide and seek, she noticed Rex was not there either, but she noticed the doorway to the passageway was open. This sent a chill down her spine like none she had ever had before. Slowly, she made her way toward the doorway. When she arrived at the door she stood at the opening looking down into the darkness and could see nothing except the first few steps made of stone. Her voice began to crack as she yelled, "Damn you Rex, if you are down there you better come back up here now or you will look like fried chicken by this time tomorrow."

As she stood at the door, she heard a faint sound like something was knocking, but it sounded very far away. Her heart began to race faster and faster just thinking of what this could be. She thought, could it be Rex down below pecking at something, or just the sounds from upstairs echoing down through the floors? She gently closed the door and went to the kitchen to find the flashlight, which was always kept in the drawer under the counter. She then made one more attempt to search the whole house for Rex, because if he was anywhere to be found she was not about to go down those stairs looking for him. Unfortunately her efforts were without reward, Rex was nowhere to be found. She then returned to the window where she had been sitting watching the snow and thought about calling over Robert or someone to go down and bring Rex upstairs. Then she turned away from the window and told herself that she must learn to do things for herself, because there may not always be someone there to do everything for her. Just like her Grams, who had lived alone with Rex for so many years, she didn't always have to call someone over to help her get him back into his cage. She thought, "If she can do it, so can I," as she slowly made her way down the hallway back toward the passageway door. She slowly pulled it back open and once again yelled down for Rex to return, but there was no answer again, only those repeated tapping sounds as if someone was knocking in the distance. One step at a time she walked slowly down the stone steps with the flashlight lighting her way, but still no sign of Rex. However, the knocking seemed much clearer now. When she had reached the bottom of the steps she was afraid to step off onto the cobblestones, because of what Robert had told her. The last thing she wanted was to end up in the middle of some Civil War battle. She stood on the last step shining the light in all directions but could not see past the wall in the first room. The door was open but she couldn't see around the corner. One thing she did know was Rex was not in this room, so he must have ventured back into one of the other rooms. She listened closely to the knocking and it sounded like it was coming from one of the other rooms through the next door, the door was open and the sound seemed to echo as to pull at her to come. Thoughts raced through her mind of turning and going back up the stairs and the hell with that damn bird, but then she thought what if he was hurt and needed help or something? She would never be able to forgive herself if she had left him down there and something was to happen to him.

Slowly, one step at a time, she placed her feet on the stones of the floor carefully, not to apply too much pressure. She thought, maybe if she was gentle it would not be enough weight to make them move. She slowly made her way over to the next room without having a problem at all and peeked around the corner with the flashlight in one hand and the newspaper in the other. It was then she noticed Rex standing, staring at the wall, with his head tilted slightly to the side as if he were listening to something. She continued to make her way toward Rex very slowly, one step at a time, and as she reached him she noticed the knocking sound was coming from the other side of the wall. This was indeed what had drawn Rex into the cobblestone room as he stood looking and listening. As the knocking continued, he tilted his head from side to side as if he was making some kind of sense of all of it. Sara placed her ear near the wall but never touched it to listen to the knocking to see if there was some kind of rhythm or message. She had decided she was not going to touch a thing, because she was afraid that something might happen. She would just wait until Norman had returned and explain to him what she had discovered while he was away. Just as she reached down and wrapped her hands around Rex to take him upstairs, Rex reached his head out and pecked on the wall. Instantly they were both pulled through the wall because she had her hands wrapped around him, sending them both into another time and place. When they stopped moving Sara and Rex found themselves inside of a wooden shed with straw scattered across the floor. In the dim lit corner of the shed sat a young woman with dark hair, curled in a bundle of fear, as tears flowed down her face. Sara was scared and confused as well at where she had ended up, and after sitting and listening to Robert's adventure, she couldn't imagine where she could be now. She approached the young woman huddled in the corner and asked, "What is your name?"

The young woman looked up to Sara and replied, "My name is Mary Parker. Who are you and how did you get in here?"

Sara answered, "I heard your knocking on the wall and when the raven touched the wall, it sent us here. Are you alright?"

Mary looked back down to the ground and said, "No, I am not alright, they are going to kill me in the morning if I do not get out of this shed before sun up."

Sara was very confused at this point and asked Mary what town she was in and if she knew what the year was as well. Mary told her that she was in Salem, Massachusetts and the year was sixteen ninety-two. This sent a cold chill once again down Sara's spine. She knew from history what that time and place represented, the Salem Witch Trials. She asked Mary why she was locked in this shed and why she was going to be killed in the morning. Mary told her that she had been found guilty of being a witch, but swore that she was not.

Mary hesitated for a second and then looked at Sara and asked, "Are you a witch?"

Sara, with a puzzled look on her face said, "No, I am not, why would you think such a thing?"

Mary replied, "Because when I banged on the wall yelling for help, the wall began to shake. Then you showed up here in this locked shed with me, with your raven. Your hair is long and black and eyes are emerald green, what would you believe if you were me?"

Sara replied, "I understand none of this makes any sense to you now, but it will in time. After all, others thought you were a witch. Was that true?"

Mary looked back into Sara's eyes and said, "What you have said is true, what one person may believe is not what makes you who you are. Our eyes and minds can be deceiving in many ways. I am sorry."

Sara told her that it was alright and now all they needed to do was get out of this shed before sun up tomorrow. It was just before sundown and Mary told her that someone would be coming soon to feed her for the last time. Sara knew that was when they would have to make their move if they were going to get away. She knew they would only be expecting one person to be in the shed when they arrived and maybe just maybe they would be able to overpower them at that time. She explained to Mary that they would have to work fast and together if this plan was going to work and to stick together if at all possible. They sat there together waiting as Mary told her about why she had been accused of being a witch. She had been helping people from time to time with cures that had been passed down through her family, many generations ago. She told her that she had helped many people through the years and then a young boy became very ill and when she tried to help him he went into convolutions and then died on her table. The young boy's family brought her up on charges of witchcraft because their son had died, and the courts found her to be guilty. Sara told her that she understood, because people fear what they do not understand and they consider that to be a threat.

Just then they heard footsteps coming from outside the shed. They knew this was going to be their only shot to get away and if they blew this chance, it was all over for both of them. As the door came open Rex took flight for the door; this was the first time he had flown since he had been injured many years ago. As he flew past the man with the food, the man fell to the ground. Sara and Mary made a dash for the door and out into the open. Sara turned as she came out the door and ran to the right, expecting Mary to follow, but she did not. She turned and ran to the left. The man who fell to the ground only noticed Sara as she ran to the right because of the confusion that was caused by Rex flying past his head. He jumped to his feet and gave chase after Sara as she tried to run for cover. Just as she reached one of the buildings, he caught her by the arm and began escorting her back to the shed. She tried to explain to him that she was not the woman they had locked inside the shed, but he wasn't buying anything she had to say. He told her that it was just another one of her tricks of witchcraft, trying to change what she looked like. When he arrived back to the shed he forced her back inside and closed the door behind her. Now all she could do was hope that Mary would come back for her during the night.

As the darkness of night slowly closed in on Sara and the shed, she had thoughts of how Rex flew away as the door came open. She knew he had to, because it was long before the accident that had caused him not to be able to fly, allowing him to fly once again. Thoughts raced through her mind wondering if Mary would return or what would become of her when the morning light finally came. The night grew longer and longer as thoughts continued to race through her mind, thoughts of Norman and all the rest of the family. She knew they had to be very concerned about her by now. She had left the door to the passageway open and was also hoping no one else would venture down those stairs searching for her. She had thought about knocking on the wall in hopes that they would be able to locate her, but she also knew this would only trap them here as well and that was the last thing she wanted. She knew Rex got her into this, now she was going to have to find the way out. As she sat there in the corner warming up with the blanket Mary had left behind, she remembered what it took for Robert to return and those thoughts were frightening to say the least. Her eyes grew tired and slowly she slipped away into sleep and was hoping when she awoke this would only have been a dream.

Soon the morning sun came shining through the slats on the shed wall catching her eyes, waking her from sleep. She knew then that Mary had not returned during the night and also this was not a dream. She feared what was to come next, as she knew they would be coming for her soon. Mary never mentioned how they planned on executing her. She peeked out through the slats on the walls, watching and looking for anything she could. It was then she saw the large pile of sticks and lumber piled around a pole that stood in the center. She also noticed a large amount of people had begun to gather to watch the judgment carried out. She thought to herself, surely they were not going burn her at the stake. She remembered the history of the Salem witch trials, and she did not remember any of them being burnt, they were all hung. Just then she heard a voice coming from the back of the shed walls, it was Mary. She had returned, but why had she waited so long? Sara ran to the back of the shed and asked her why they were going to burn her. Mary told her they had already tried to hang her, but she was able to set herself free from the rope and get away, just to be caught again later by the search party that continued to hunt her down. They figured that if they surrounded her with fire she would have no place to run. It was then that Mary told her she indeed was a witch and that was how she had freed herself from the rope. At this point Sara was not concerned about if Mary was a witch or not, all she wanted to do was get out of this shed.

Sara told Mary that she needed to get out of here now, before someone came for her. She then told her to pull on the slat as she pushed from the inside. Together they were able to pull one of the slats from the wall loose, but the opening was still too small for Sara to fit through.

Sara asked, "If you are a witch, why didn't you set yourself free from the shed?"

Mary answered, "Because I had a locket that I wore around my neck, it was passed down to me from my mother and her mother as well, it holds the power of the spells I used to escape and vanish. They took it away from me before they placed me into the shed."

Sara asked, "Where is the locket now and how did it work?"

Mary answered, "I do not know what they have done with the locket, but all you needed to do was to hold it in your hand and think of where you wanted to be and it would happen."

Together both of them tried with all of their might to pull another board free from the wall, but were unable to do so. It was then Sara heard someone coming. She could also hear the crowd, as they became more eager to watch the show. She heard the boards on the door as they were being removed and turned and looked back for Mary, but she was off and running. She saw Mary turn the corner to hide behind one of the other buildings in the distance. Two men entered the shed together and each took Sara by an arm and escorted her out of the shed and into the light of the morning sun. As the two men continued walking her toward the large pile of lumber, the crowd began to roar louder and louder as if they were getting excited about what was about to happen. Sara found it hard to believe that anyone could enjoy watching the pain and suffering of another soul. Step by step she came closer to the pile of lumber hoping something would happen to send her back where she belonged, but nothing happened. Her greatest fear was coming true, the sentence was going to be carried out, even though she was not Mary. The two men walked her through a clearing and to the pole that stood in the center of the pile of wood and bound her to the pole with her hands bound in front of her. An old man who looked to be wearing the robe of a judge of some sort walked up to her and explained to her she was to be put to death by fire and that her hands were free to pray if she wanted to ask for forgiveness. Sara tried to explain to the elderly man that she was not Mary at all and that she was not from this place. It was as if he was not hearing a word she had to say. She figured they were afraid to listen because they were afraid she would place a spell on them and blind them from what they felt was the truth. The truth was they knew nothing of the truth at all.

Sara stood tied to the pole unsure of what was going to become of her, knowing that her family had to be very worried about where she had made off to. She was sure that they would notice Rex was gone as well and put two and two together, knowing he had once again played a part in the disappearance. She then noticed the roar of the crowd began to build as the two men who had escorted her to the pole walked toward the pile of lumber, both carrying a torch to light the fire. Both men started at opposite sides of the pile and worked their way around the circle until they had the entire radius burning. The fire would take a while to build enough to get to her, but she was growing very nervous just the same. Slowly the flames grew higher and higher and she was starting to feel the heat as she tried to shield her face from the flames. Then she noticed something in the distant sky, coming toward her at a very fast pace. Whatever it was grew closer and closer as the flames grew higher. Then, as it came bursting through the flames, it was clear to see that it was indeed Rex. He flew through flames and landed on her shoulder and she noticed something hanging from his beak. She reached up with her hands bound together and took it from him. It was then she knew it was the locket that

Mary had told her about. As the flames grew higher and hotter she placed the locket between her hands and did just as Mary had described, she wished she was back where she had come from, safe from the fire and death. The flames flashed high into the air and then disappeared from the pile of lumber as if they had never been lit at all. The pole stood tall in the center, but Sara and Rex had vanished into thin air.

In a matter of seconds, Sara and Rex found themselves standing along side of the wall that had taken them to another place and time. Rex's wings were a little burnt on the edges from flying through the flames and the smoke was still rising off of Sara's clothing. She was afraid to move but Rex was not, so he hopped across the floor, once again unable to fly from his old injury. He stopped to look back to make sure Sara knew to follow carefully behind. Each stone that Rex stepped upon, Sara was careful to follow, until they had returned to the stone stairway once again. When they arrived back to the top of the stairway they noticed that the door was still open, then carefully, they walked down the hallway and as they entered into the kitchen there sat Norman, Robert and her sister Susan at the old wooden table that was fastened to the floor. You could have knocked them all over with a feather as they jumped from the table and saw Sara and Rex standing there as smoke rose from the both of them. Sara sat down at the table and began telling them all about what had happened as Rex scampered off out of sight to search for a whole new adventure. Robert headed him off before he could make his way back down the stairs and then closed and sealed the door. He then corralled Rex back to his cage where he would be safe and sound and so would everyone else as long as he remained there. One thing for certain, was Rex had taken Sara to this strange place in time, but he had also saved her from the fire.

Norman told her he had returned late last night to find the doorway to the stone steps open and was afraid that she and Rex had ventured down the stairs for some reason, not understanding what that could have been. He then contacted Robert and Susan and they had come right over and had been there all night waiting and hoping for her to return. Robert had gone down the stairs looking for a sign of her and Rex but nothing was to be found, Susan on the other hand had told them both there was no way she was going down into the dungeon no matter what ever happened. Just the thought of it gave her cold chills all the way to the bone.

Sara sat there at the table that day telling her tale of the shed and Mary. She opened her hand and from her fingertips dangled the locket that had brought her home. From that day forth she would always wonder what had become of Mary and had placed the locket gently into her jewelry box for safe keeping, never knowing when it may come in handy once again. Because she knew only time would tell how many secrets and adventures those stone walls could hold for them all.

The Light

The harshness of winter had finally passed, it had been one of the most brutal winters that anyone in these parts could remember. It snowed for days and days, never seeming to end, but now the fresh warm breeze of spring was in the air. It would be some time before the rivers and streams would return back to their normal levels and the spring rains would cause flooding for many. Norman stood outside on this warm spring morning taking in the crisp fresh air as if it were the first breath of spring to hit his lungs. As he opened his eyes he spotted a small moth that was circling just a few feet from him and then vanished off into the air as quickly as it had appeared. He thought to himself about how precious life is and how fragile it can be, but to him this was a sign that spring brought new life and a new beginning for all living things. This was by far his favorite time of the year; when the flowers began to bloom and the singing of the birds of spring brought music to his ears, it was as if his friends had returned.

Today Norman had the day to himself, his darling wife Sara had went off shopping with her sister Susan; they had went down to the docks to gather up the fresh fruits and vegetables and would always come back to divide them up with their neighbors and family. Susan didn't care much for hanging around this old house because there was something about it that just gave her the creeps and would send cold chills down her spine. She didn't think it was because of the cobblestone room because she had these feelings long before the room was discovered. However, it was something she would overlook to be with the family, but there was no way she was going to be there alone. She wasn't quite sure what it was about the place that bothered her, but she knew there was something. The place seemed to be more suited for a museum than a home to her because it was large and historical in many ways. She loved the old place, just wouldn't want to ever live there.

As the morning passed, Norman walked about the estate with his dog, tossing his ball, playing together as they always did. As he gazed up to the sky he noticed the clouds had started to build and it was getting dark pretty fast. This was normal in the spring, as the moisture would rise from the heating of the sun. As the air would warm, a spring thunderstorm would develop rather quickly. His first thought was that he was a little concerned because Sara and Susan had not returned. He knew they would be all right, it was just that normal feeling a husband has about protecting and caring for those he loves. He thought he'd better secure things just in case the winds started to pick up as it usually did in these parts. As he was finishing he noticed the clouds were getting a little darker and darker by the second as he stood looking, then a flash of lightning shot across the sky, like fingers on a hand. He knew this was going to be a bad one, so he whistled for his old buddy to go inside while there was still time. He only hoped that Sara and Susan got home before things got any worse, but they did not. They no sooner got inside and all hell broke loose, the rain came pounding down and the winds grew stronger and stronger, with lightning flashing all across the sky. As he stood there looking out the windows he couldn't help but think of the small moth he had seen earlier and wondered where he was now. He knew just as fast as nature can begin life, it can take it away in the twinkling of an eye.

He sat there in the window with his eyes closed listening to the rain as it tapped against the window and thought to himself how peaceful nature's sounds can be. It had been a while since he had heard anything from Rex and he thought he had better check on him just in case the storm had frightened him in some way. It was no big surprise to Norman when he walked into the room and found Rex's cage empty once again. It seemed it didn't matter what they did to try to lock his door to his cage, this bird was like Houdini and would always find a way to get out. Norman always planned on setting up a video camera, just so they could see how he always escaped. Norman knew the first place to look for Rex was the doorway to the Cobblestone room. That is where he would always seem to go when he would get out, so all they would have to do was corral him back to the den and into his cage most of the time. As Norman made his way through the house the lightning flashed with all of its might and all the power in the house went out. That was not a good thing because it was not going to make it any easier to find Rex if he was not in his usual place, standing at the door. Not to mention this crazy bird gave him the creeps in the light, and the darkness wasn't going to make things any better. As Norman turned the corner sure as could be there stood Rex gazing at the passageway door, waiting for it to open. The only thing was for some reason there was light shining through from the other side, all around the edges of the door. Norman stopped and wondered how this was possible, if all the power was off in the house because of the storm. He stood there just like Rex and looked at the door as if he thought for some reason it was about to open, but it did not. All kinds of things raced through his mind as he stood there waiting, wondering what to do. It was then that a thought flashed through his mind, what if it is a fire down stairs? He knew right then and there he had better check it out. The last thing he wanted to do while he was there alone was to open that door but he knew he had no choice. He looked down at old Rex and said, "Listen you over-sized pigeon, don't take off down there when I open the door this time."

As soon as he pulled the door open far enough for Rex to get through he bolted through the opening and down the stone steps and into the light. Norman stood at the top of the steps and yelled for Rex as if he really thought that was going to do any good. He could not see where the light was coming from where he was standing and knew he had no choice but to investigate further. But before he did, he went to get his jacket, because he knew no matter how warm it was outside, it always seemed to be cold down in the cobblestone rooms. When he returned, he made his way slowly down the steps and he could now see where the light was coming from, it was a single stone that seemed to be glowing very bright. Rex stood just to the side of it and was gazing into it as if he could see something moving, like a crystal ball of some sort. The closer Norman came to this stone the brighter it seemed to glow, as if it were on fire. He knelt down on one knee next to Rex to see if he could see anything, but the light was much too bright for his eyes. It didn't seem to bother Rex however; it was as if he were watching something very carefully. Norman wondered if it was hot so he closed his eyes and reached out with his hand to feel if there was any heat rising from the stone and just as he put his hand in the light, he was gone and so was the light. Rex stood there looking at the stone for a few moments and then scampered off and up the stairs nudging the door closed with his beak and back to his cage, where he felt safe.

With his eyes clinched tight, Norman was surprised to feel such a cold feeling as if a very cold wind had rushed past him and his hand seemed very cold. As he opened his eyes he realized he was not in the cobblestone room any longer, he had somehow been thrust into a cold and windy winter night. He couldn't help but wonder where he might be, but by the look of things he figured it had to be at least sixty or seventy years back in time. It was late at night and there was very little movement on the streets, but he could tell that he was in a large city. He couldn't seem to put his finger on where this place could be, but there was something about it that brought him peace. He was sure glad he had gone back for his jacket before he ventured down those steps because no matter where he was now it was bone chillingly cold. He figured the temperatures had to be in the teens and would probably get colder as the night went on. He noticed down at the far end of the alley there was a fire barrel burning and a few men standing around it trying to stay warm. He made his way down the alley and asked the men if they would mind if he shared their fire to warm his bones. They both smiled and told him the fire was free and that he was welcome to join them.

As Norman stood looking into the barrel he couldn't help but notice something strange burning in the barrel and asked, "What are you burning?"

One of the men answered, "Records."

Norman looked into the face of the man who had answered and he was a tall thin black man with a weathered look on his face. Loving music the way that he did, Norman couldn't help but ask, "What kind of records might they have been?"

The man answered, "We are musicians and the records were jazz."

Norman asked, "Why are you burning all of your records?"

62 / James H. Pierce

The man looked into Norman's eyes and said, "The records are no good to any of us now, no one has the money to buy such things. We figure at least they can keep us warm this cold and winter night."

Norman felt his heart sink knowing all of these records must have meant very much to these men and said, "I seem to be a little confused, can you tell me where I am and what the date may be today."

One of the men answered, "You are in the city of Chicago, January twenty third, nineteen thirty two."

Norman kindly thanked him and he knew it meant he had probably been thrust into a cold and winter night during the Great Depression. Being a musician himself he knew the history of what the depression had meant and done to not only the music world but to everyone. It was a great time of suffering, hunger and sadness for all. Not sure why he had been sent here, he couldn't help but wonder what was to become of him on this cold and winter night. As the fire in the barrel slowly came to an end the two men bid him good luck and slowly walked out of the alley and out to the streets. He found himself a little confused on what to do next and as he turned to walk away, he heard what sounded like a cough coming from under a pile of newspapers. As he pulled the papers slowly from the pile he found an old man shivering, he then pulled his jacket off and wrapped it around the old man in an attempt to warm him. But he knew it was going to take much more than what he had to keep him warm on this cold and winter night. He had asked the man if he had eaten anything today and he told him that he had not eaten in several days. Norman wrapped him back in the papers and told him that he would return soon with something for him to eat. Now freezing, he ran from the alley and into the street hoping to find anyone who may be willing to offer him help, but it was late and the streets were bare. He noticed up the street there was a diner and when he arrived to the front door he noticed they were closed, but could see a light in the back room. He knocked on the door, but no one came to answer, so he ran to the back of the building and pounded on the back door, just praying for someone to answer.

Through the door there was a voice that said, "The diner is closed."

Norman pressed his face against the door and yelled, "Please, I need your help, there is a man laying in the alley starving and freezing to death."

For a few seconds there was no sound at all, then the door came open and there stood a woman who looked to be very old, her hair was white as snow. She shouted, "Quickly, come inside and close the door."

Once inside, he thanked her and told her about the man that he had found out in the alley. She never said a word she just scampered off into the kitchen and returned with a pie pan full of food and a blanket across her arm. She told him to take these things and as he turned to walk away she noticed he himself was not wearing a coat at all. She told him to wait and scampered off once again, this time she returned with a coat that was large enough for him to wear. He thanked her very much and told her that he would repay her some how when he was able. She told him that it was not necessary because the food was left from the day and the coat had been left there for some time by one of the customers who never returned. She told him that the Lord had blessed her through these bad times and kept her doors open and she felt the least she could do was to help others who were not so fortunate. He smiled and thanked her kindly and she opened the door and he walked back out into the alley once again.

Norman returned to the alley where the man had been sleeping and pulled the papers from him once again. He sat him up and began feeding him the food the woman had given to him as he wrapped the blanket around his shoulders.

The man stopped short of eating all the food and looked to Norman and said, "The rest is for you my friend, and I thank you very much for your kindness."

Norman answered, "No, the food is all for you tonight, you need your strength to stay warm."

The man finished eating the plate of food and thanked Norman for all he had done to help him. Norman just smiled and told him he felt that he had been sent here to help him on this cold and winter night. The old man looked at Norman wondering what he could have meant by what he had just said and why anyone would be sent to help him. Norman then carefully covered the man with the papers that he had been using to stay warm. He then sat down beside him against the brick wall, pulling the coat closed the kind old woman had given to him to stay warm. He sat there through most of the night growing colder and colder, feeling the pain that only cold can do to a body. He felt himself trying to fall to sleep and struggled to stay awake, fearing if he slipped off, he may freeze to death and never wake again. Soon the pain was gone and he could not fight the closing of his eyes any longer, he slipped off into the night, to be awaked by warmth and light all around himself. As he tried to get to his feet he was greeted by many in which he had not seen in years, then it dawned on him, these were all people who had left his world and gone to be with God. They gathered all around him and guided him down a long passageway and before a light so bright that it consumed his very soul. From this light a voice rang out, a voice so comforting and loving, like nothing he had ever heard before.

The voice rang out, "Welcome to my home Norman, I have brought you here to thank you for all that you have done."

Norman humbly asked, "Have I passed into the night and is this heaven that I have found; Is that you Lord?"

The voice answered, "Yes it is I, this is Heaven. Your time has not come for you to join us here, because your work is not complete."

Norman asked, "Then why have you brought me here if it is not my time to stay?"

The voice rang out from the light once again and said, "I have brought you here to protect you, as you have done for others. You have given your own life to save another, there is no greater honor that you can show me."

Norman asked, "I simply found myself there not knowing how or why, I simply have done what all should do."

The voice answered, "Yes, you have done what all should do to help others. All that have passed through the cobblestone rooms have all reached out to help or comfort others. These rooms are found nowhere else on Earth and only those who are chosen find their way to the proper stones."

Norman asked, "Could you tell me something, does Rex play a part in all of this?"

The sound of laughter rang out from the light as the Lord answered, "Yes, all living creatures belong to me and it is I who unlocks his cage, to send him on his way."

Norman asked, "May I also ask what has happened to the man in the alley?"

The Lord softly answered, "When the morning sun rises this morning, he will awaken and rise to his feet. Because of the kindness that you have shown him, in his life he will reach out to help thousands of people who are in need and save many lives. He feels that you were an angel that had been sent to him this night, and you have given him the will to not only live, but to give life to others."

Norman stood there with tears of joy trickling down his face for what he had done, voice cracking with emotions he said, "Thank you Lord, for all that you have done."

The Lord answered, "No, my son, thank you for all that you have done. Through you and all of those like yourself my will is done and through all of you I am given hope for all of mankind. Now I give you this night to spend time with all of those you love here and then as quickly as you have come to this place you shall leave."

Norman thanked the Lord for everything and promised to continue to do his good will for all of those whose paths he crossed, and the brightness of the light slowly slipped away. He was once again surrounded by all of those who had passed into the light. Some of which he had never even met, but yet in some small way he had made a difference in their lives as well. It was clear to him then that there are so many small things that we never give a thought about doing, that effect so many lives in so many ways.

Back at home Sara and Susan had returned several hours after Norman had entered the room, not knowing he had ventured down into the cobblestone room at all. They had searched the house and grounds for him, but he was nowhere to be found. They noticed that Rex was safe in his cage and the doorway to the cobblestone rooms was closed, not to mention they knew Norman would have never ventured down those steps alone. They had become very concerned because when they arrived at the house the power was still off and he was nowhere to be found. It was not like him at all to leave without telling someone or leaving a note for someone to find. All that day and into the night they hoped to hear from him or for his return, but that did not happen. Even though Susan was terrified to stay in the home over night, she stayed with Sara this night waiting for word from her Norman, but there was none. Sometime during the night they had both slipped off to sleep sitting at the old wooden table in the kitchen.

Soon the morning sun began to peek out from the horizon and the morning sky began to glow with light, bringing on a new day of life. But deep into the darkness of the cobblestone room Norman lay on the floor sleeping like a baby. The next thing he knew someone was tapping him on the check and calling out his name. When he opened his eyes he was very surprised to see that it was old Red standing there with a lantern from so long ago in his hand.

Norman asked him what he was doing there and he told him he thought it was time to come home to see his mother before her time here had passed, and to see his old friend Jim once again. Red asked Norman what he was doing down here laying on the floor and Norman started telling him of what he had seen and where he had been. Red stood there in the light of the lantern and listened to every word that came from Norman's mouth, knowing every word to be true.

Red said to Norman, "This room is no mystery, each stone holds an answer or a direction in our lives. We can step upon these stones many, many times and never see a thing, but when the time is right, worlds will open up to us so we can see what we are meant to see.

Norman looked at Red and said, "I've lived here many years and never knew this room was here at all and then just as you have said, it was all exposed for us to see."

Red answered, "Yes, I believe we will never know all the adventures that these rooms will truly hold."

Norman asked, "Will you return to your place in the past after you see your Mother and Jim?"

Red answered, "No, my place is here now, I have done what I was sent to do and the Lord came to me in my sleep and told me to return. I will not be going back again, I am home to stay."

Red helped Norman to his feet and they made their way up the cobblestone steps and forced the door open. As they made their way down the hallway and to the kitchen, they found Sara and Susan sitting at the old wooden table drinking a cup of hot tea. Susan jumped from her seat as if she had seen a ghost and yelled, "I hate it the way everyone in this house keeps appearing and disappearing without warning.'

Norman and Red both burst out into laughter knowing how much this place gave her the creeps. Sara jumped up from the table and wrapped her arms around Norman and hugged him with all her might. He told her that he was sorry that she had to worry about him and that he had much to tell her about his adventure. She knew from her own adventure that she was just glad he was able to return safely. Norman offered Red something to eat and a cup of tea, but Red told him thanks, all he wanted to do was get moving because he had a long way to go. Norman stopped him and told him that Jim had returned about a year ago and left a car out in the shed for him just in case he ever returned. Then he handed him enough money for gas to get himself home safely and shook his hand and thanked him for helping him this morning when he returned. Red told him that he believed he was meant to be there to wake him and help him to his feet this morning and that he was grateful to the Lord for that.

Norman, Sara and Susan stood at the driveway and watched as Red drove around the corner and out of sight. They returned inside to the table as Norman began telling them both about what he had seen and where he had been. He told them about how the power had gone off and how the stone seemed to glow from the floor. Susan wasn't too sure she wanted to hear much more, because she already could feel the hair moving as if someone was breathing down the back of her neck. Norman told them that when Red had awakened him from the floor he couldn't help but wonder if some how it was all a dream. It was then Sara asked him where he had gotten the coat. As he looked down at himself he noticed that it was the coat that the old woman from the diner had given him. A smile came across his face like no other, because he knew he had stood before the Lord and this was not a dream at all. One thing he knew for sure was he never going to be able to look at Rex or the cobblestone room the same way again.

The Calling

The days have become longer as summer slowly slipped its way into the changing of the seasons. The nights seemed to become warmer and warmer as the cool spring nights became a thing of the past, at least for the next several months. Tonight the air seemed to be a little more humid than most, maybe because the air was so still. Susan stood quietly as she watched the sun slowly slip behind the horizon and evening took charge of the day. As she stood there thinking about her life, the phone inside began to ring. She was in no hurry to answer it because she was enjoying the view. She figured who ever it was would call back or the answering machine would pick it up. As she stood there listening to the phone, the ringing never stopped, it seemed to go on and on as if someone was trying very hard to get in contact with her. She turned and walked back inside and by now she had figured the phone had to have rang fifteen to twenty times at least, and was still ringing as if there would be no end. The thing she could not understand was why her answering machine was not picking up on the call. As she stood looking down at the phone she noticed the answering machine was on but was not doing its job. She also noticed the number on the caller ID was no other than

Sara and Norman's home. As she noticed the number she grabbed the phone quickly, hoping to catch them before they hung up. She picked up the phone and said, "Hello, this is Susan", but there was no answer, only the sound of silence as a cold chill ran down her spine. She hung up the phone and called the number back, but it was busy. She couldn't imagine what could be happening or why they would call and then be busy when she called right back. The more she sat there thinking about it the more concerned she became, as all kinds of thoughts raced through her mind about how spooky their house was to her.

Susan grabbed her purse and keys to the car and out the door she ran, heading for the old estate where Sara and Norman lived. The farther she drove the more the sky darkened and she could see flashes of lightning in the distance. The closer she came to the old estate the more the lightning flashed across the sky. As she pulled through the gates of the old estate the rain began to fall from the sky with a fury. She pulled down the long drive and to the house and waited for the rain to slow before making a dash inside. She felt as if some strange force was trying to keep her from going inside, but just as fast as the rain had started there was a pause and that was when she made her move for the door. She reached for the door and was very surprised to find it unlocked and open as if someone had opened the door expecting her arrival. She walked inside she shouted several times for anyone who may have been inside, but there was no answer to be heard. She made her way through the house looking for any sign of anyone or anything she could feel the fear over take her and her heart began to pound as if it were going to jump out of her chest. As she came around the corner and into the den it was then that the hair stood up on the back of her neck. There stood Rex looking down at the phone on the table with his head turned slightly to the side as if he were listening as it lay there off of the hook. Susan was a little afraid of Rex, but slowly reached over and picked up the phone to see if there was someone there, but all she heard once again was silence. She hung up the phone and pressed redial to find out where the last call would have been to. It was no surprise to her at all when her answering machine picked up on the other end. What she couldn't understand was why it was working now but would not work earlier when the call was first made.

As she stood there looking at Rex, he stood there looking back at her as if he had something he would have said if he were able, but not a sound, only his persistent stare. She could tell by the look in his eyes that he was up to something and she thought to herself that she wasn't going to fall for his antics like the others had. She looked at Rex and shouted, "There is no way you are getting me to go down into that old stone room and off into one of your crazy adventures."

Rex just stood there and then looked down as if he were pouting and then back up and stared at her as he took in every word she was saying. He then slowly turned and began walking away from the phone, looking back after a few steps as if he were expecting Susan to follow, or something else to happen. After a few moments the phone began to ring as Rex stopped in his tracks and turned to look at Susan as if to see what she would do next. She stood there looking down at the phone, afraid to answer it, but also afraid that if she didn't she may miss an important call that would explain exactly what was going on. She slowly reached down after the third ring and placed her hand on the receiver, but couldn't make herself pick it up for some reason. She glanced over at Rex to see what he was doing and he was standing there with his head tilted slightly to the left as though he was waiting to see what she would do next. The way he looked at her sent cold chills down her spine, as she grasped the receiver tighter in her hand. Now the phone had reached the sixth ring and she knew she had to make up her mind right here and now if she was going to accept this call. As the seventh ring rang out in the room she slowly lifted the receiver from the base and placed it to her ear and said nothing, she just listened to see if there was anyone on the other end. It was then that the line went dead and the receiver fell to the side of the table and Susan had vanished from the spot she was standing. Rex now cocked his head from left to right and then turned to walk away as if his job was done.

It took a few moments for Susan to realize what had happened. She found herself standing on a trail deep within the woods and as she looked down she also noticed her clothes had changed from when she was standing in the den and had answered the phone. She was now wearing a long dress that reached the ground, something she thought to herself would have been worn many, many years ago. As fear raced through her mind she couldn't help but wonder where she could have ended up. After hearing all of the things the others had seen and been through, she could only imagine what was in store for her. She stood there looking around trying to think about what she should do next and she could hear the birds singing in the trees, but off in the distance she could hear what appeared to be the muffled sounds of a young child crying. Being the caring woman that she was, she forgot about where she was for the moment and started trying to locate where this child might be and see if there was anything she could do to help. About one hundred yards up the path she came across a young black girl about six years old, she was curled up along side of a tree. As she reached down and touched her, the young girl jumped to her feet and began to rub her eyes as if she had been startled. Susan told her in a very soft voice that she was not going to hurt her and all she wanted to do was help her if she could. The young girl stopped rubbing her eyes

Fisherman's Fog / 75

and reached out and wrapped her arms around Susan's legs squeezing her long dress tightly around them. Susan stood there and rubbed her hand gently across the young girl's head until she had settled a bit.

As the young girl slowly released Susan's legs she looked up to her with big tears still in her eyes. Susan bent down to her and asked her what was the matter and why she was out here in the woods all alone and crying. The young girl, who was still having a hard time talking after crying, mumbled out the words, "They took my Mommy and Daddy away."

Susan was now not only confused about where she was, but was now also confused about why anyone would take this young girl's parents away and leave her alone in the woods. She placed the young girl's face gently between her hands and lifted her face up so she could look into her eyes and said, "Do not be afraid, I will stay with you and try to help you find your parents. Now do you know why they took your Mommy and Daddy away?"

The little girl shook her head yes and then replied, "My Daddy was taking us to a place where he heard we could be free and these bad men were trying to stop us from getting there. My mommy told me to run and to hide until the bad men were gone and when I came out my mommy and daddy were gone and I could not find them anywhere."

Susan wrapped her arms around her and hugged her for a few moments until she felt the little girl stop shaking and then asked, "Which way were you walking on the path before the bad men came along?"

The little girl pointed to the right and now at least Susan had some idea which direction she should be going. After all, the only thing she knew at this point was they were running from something and she thought in the back of her mind it could only be slavery. By the look of the clothes that she was wearing it would fit right in with the time period that the little girl may be talking about. Susan looked back into the little girl's eyes and she could see her fears starting to fade just a bit and the crying had come to a stop. It was then she asked, "And what might this pretty little girl's name be?"

The little girl smiled and answered, "Tonya, my name is Tonya."

Susan smiled and told her that it was a very pretty name and took Tonya by the hand. It was then she noticed she had the chain of a necklace in her hand. She asked Tonya what it was she was carrying and she raised it up for Susan to see. It was a beautiful broach and chain and she told her that her mother gave it to her to hold as they walked through the woods. Susan told her she thought it was beautiful and that her mother would be proud of her because she had not lost it.

They waited patiently for a few moments listening for any sound of anyone coming and then began walking down the path in the direction that her parents had been going before the bad men had come along. She was also hoping those same men didn't come back before she found out where the path would lead her and Tonya. It only took a few moments down the path before she spotted something off into the trees and she knew what it was and directed Tonya's attention away from seeing it as they passed the area. It was her mother and father, they had been left hanging in the trees for anyone else who may have the same idea to come along and see what fate they would meet. Susan did her best to fight off the tears and pain of sorrow because she was trying to not let on to Tonya. She didn't want her to see her parents like that and remember it for the rest of her life. She held her hand very tight and drifted from the path and down the hill into the trees, and then circled back around to the path farther through the woods, where her parents could not be seen.

For the next hour they stuck to the path and never saw or heard another soul. They only heard the sound of the woods, the birds chirping and squirrels barking in the trees as the wind made a rustling sound in the leaves surrounding them as they walked the path. It was then that Susan saw the clearing ahead and she was relieved to know they were going to make it out of the woods before sunset. She wasn't too sure she was going to be able to take a night in the woods. After all, she didn't even like camping and wouldn't have had the slightest idea how to start a fire by rubbing two sticks together.

As the two of them reached the edge of the tree line they could see large fields with people out working in them, and then way off into the distance Susan could see a large white house with many smaller buildings off further in the distance. She knew this was their only chance at shelter if they were going to find it before dark, so with feet aching and legs beginning to cramp they pushed on toward the big white house. An old black gentleman came running from the field where he had been working and greeted them as they went past the fields. He welcomed them both and offered them a drink of water that he was carrying in a leather pouch around his waist. They both took a drink from the pouch and thanked him very much for being so kind. Tonya asked the man if he had seen her mommy and daddy and he looked up at Susan and then looked back down to Tonya and told her no, but maybe she could check up at the house with Mr. Abernathy. He told her that many people come past that he does not see while working, but they all stop to see Mr. Abernathy before passing, because there was not another plantation or house for many miles. Susan kindly thanked him again for the water and his time and walked away toward the big white house. She had hopes that Mr. Abernathy would be able to give them shelter for the night and maybe answer a few questions about where she might be now. She knew just like all of those who had been sent on one of these journeys that there was a mission or a lesson to be learned before she would be able to return and she knew in her heart it could not be as simple as finding Tonya and getting her to safety.

As they made their way closer to the large white plantation home Tonya squeezed Susan's hand a little harder with anticipation that maybe her parents would be here waiting for her. But Susan knew that Tonya was never going to see her parents again and this just broke her heart. She knew that not only would Tonya never see her parents again, she knew it was best if she never knew what had happened to them as well. All she could do now was to hope to find a home or a safe place for her, where she would have the chance to be free, the gift her father and mother perished trying to give to her.

When the two of them arrived at the front of the house they were greeted with open arms by an elderly gentleman with long snow white hair and a mustache and beard to match. He had such a kind and gentle look about him, but yet strong and comforting as well.

He walked down the steps to greet them and said, "Welcome to my home, we call this place Freedom and my name is Jacob Abernathy. What brings me the pleasure of your visit?"

Susan was not quite sure how to begin her story. Knowing not only would her tale of how she got here be alarming, she also felt there was not much of a chance of him believing her or understanding it any better than she did. She politely introduced Tonya and then herself to Mr. Abernathy, as he stood there with a pleasant smile upon his face. Then a young black woman came through the front door carrying a pitcher of lemonade and two glasses and sat them upon a table. The table sat neatly on the front porch, where the over hang on the porch protected them from the sun. The young woman then came over to Tonya and reached out for her hand and asked her if she would like to come inside with her and look around a bit. Tonya released Susan's hand and took the hand of the young woman and scampered off into the house for a look around. Jacob politely asked Susan if she would honor him in sitting and having a cool glass of lemonade with him and tell him about how she came across his plantation. She smiled and accepted his invitation, but she wasn't quite sure how or where she would begin. As Jacob poured her a glass of lemonade he asked her where she was from and what she had seen along her journey. She told him she was from a place very far away from here and that she had came across Tonya in the woods just a few hours from his plantation. Then she explained to him what had happened to her parents along the way and how she had told Tonya that her parents were taking her to a place to live freely. Jacob looked down as Susan told him the story and when he looked up at her he had tears in his eyes and she could tell that he was very touched by what she had just told him. He sat there for a moment and then told her that this is the place they were trying to find and how it saddened his heart to know they had come so far and made it so close before their journey had ended. Susan said she did not understand why someone would carry so much hatred for another human being and why it meant so much to them to stop someone else from being free. Jacob looked into her eyes and asked her where it was that she said she was from, because he found it strange for a woman of her age and race to believe and say the things she was saying during this time and in the area they lived in.

Susan hesitated for a moment and then thought it was time to explain all she knew about how she got here and where she was from. She explain that she was from a time long into the future and how many had made these trips before to serve a purpose and never knew where or why they were sent to these places. But when they were through and returned, they understood what it was they were sent there for; it was to help others along the way. Jacob listened to every word that crossed her lips with amazement, and never once did he seem to disbelieve or have a reason to doubt what she was saying. After all it was clear from the start that she was not from these parts, she talked so much differently than others and she seemed to be educated and carry herself with confidence. These were not things he had seen in many women.

He wanted to know more about where she had come from and what the future would hold for all of the people that he tried so desperately to help here at his plantation. She told him that she did not know what would happen to all of those that he tried so much to help, but she told him that times would eventually change and people would be free of slavery and will be given the same rights as others. This brought a smile to his face, just knowing that maybe somewhere along the line through all of history maybe, just maybe he and his father played a part in freedom for all.

Jacob sat there sipping on his lemonade and thought it was his turn to explain where he was now and what he figured his goal and purpose was in life. He told her that this was his father's plantation and how they had lived there all of their lives. He explained to her how his father used to go to the harbor and buy the slaves that came in that seemed to be abused and neglected. He was doing his best to keep the whole family together if possible. Many times he told her this was not possible because they had been separated before coming here. Then how his father would hear a slave was being mistreated or abused at another plantation and how he would travel many miles to make an offer to purchase them and their family, to come and work on his farm with him. Many, many years ago his father had passed away and his one dying wish was for him to continue with this work, and how proud he was to have been able to keep his promise.

Susan couldn't help but ask, "What are you trying to do by bringing them back here to work instead of where they had been before? They are still slaves aren't they?"

Jacob smiled and shook his head and replied, "No Ma'am, everyone here on this farm is free and they all share equally in what we do here, that was my father's wish. Each family has their own house as I am sure you saw on the way in from the fields, and they also share equally in everything we harvest here at the plantation without fear of being hung or murdered for being free."

Susan couldn't help but ask, "Hasn't anyone ever come and tried to stop you from what it is you are doing or considered what you are doing a threat to their own way of life?"

Once again Jacob smiled and said, "Yes, several times before many men have gathered and come to try to destroy what we have here. But unlike most farms and places where slavery exists, the people who live here have something to fight for and that is freedom for them and their families and we are of such great numbers it would take whole armies to defeat us now. They have tried many times and have been forced back with many losses and in time they have learned to just leave us alone and act as if we do not exist."

This brought very much comfort to Susan as she sat and listened to his words and then she asked, "What about Tonya's parents? They are hanging a few miles back into the woods. What are we going to do about that? How could that happen?"

With sadness in his eyes he turned his head both ways making sure no one was near. Then he whispered softly so Tonya would not over hear, "We will take a large group of men in the morning and cut them down and give them a proper burial. They know they cannot stop them once they have come here, so they have patrols that watch the paths to cut them down before they reach us. There is not a lot that we can do about that, some make it through and others do not. It is impossible for us to protect them all because they come to us from so many different places and directions at times, but we do the best we can."

The sun was slowly starting to set and the workers were making their way back from the fields. As each one passed by the porch where they were sitting, they smiled and waved one by one and said goodnight to Mr. Abernathy. You could see the love and respect that they had for this charming man. He sat there watching as all of the workers slowly made their way back to their home. After the last one had passed for the evening, he looked at Susan and told her that it was time to go in and see if they could get her settled for the night. Susan thought to herself how lucky she was to have stumbled onto this plantation and to have found the safe haven that Tonya's parents had sought out for her. It was as if her hand and legs were guided by the Lord and for the first time she was no longer afraid of what she may face next along her adventure.

As the sun fell behind the horizon, darkness came very quickly. Jacob picked up the oil lamp and lit it, turned to Susan and offered to show her to her room. Susan was very impressed with the beauty of his home and how well it had been taken care of. She was never much on big old houses because for some reason they normally gave her the creeps. She didn't know why but for some reason she felt very comfortable here. As Jacob opened the door to the room where she would be sleeping it was as if she had entered a fairy tale or something, everything was perfect, all white and trimmed in lace, with a feather bed mattress and pillows to match. He then walked her over to the French doors that led to the balcony out back and the view was breathtaking.

She could stand right there on the balcony and see all of the homes of all the workers and as their lamps lit up their homes she could hear laughter and joy coming across the lawn. She then understood why it was worth risking their lives to have a chance at this life they called freedom. Jacob excused himself from her room and as he was leaving he turned and asked her is she would join him for supper in about half an hour. She agreed that would be very nice and thanked him kindly for everything.

After about ten minutes there was a knock at her door and when she opened it, there stood an elderly black woman with a most beautiful dress across her arms. She told Susan that the dress was for her to wear down to dinner and as soon as she had changed they would be ready for her. Susan asked where they had taken Tonya, and the elderly woman told her that she had been given a room of her own and would be joining them for dinner as well. The elderly woman closed the door and Susan raced off to change her clothes and make her way downstairs where everyone would be waiting for her to arrive.

As she made her way downstairs she couldn't help but notice the dinning table was set most elegantly and there were many places set for many people to be served; The china plates all neatly in their places and crystal glasses for all. She was the first to arrive to the table so Jacob stood and walked over and pulled her chair from the table to help her to her seat. She found it so hard to believe here in the middle of nowhere everything could be so perfect. One dish at a time the servants brought the food to the table and when they were through there seemed to be enough food placed on this table to feed an army. Then she noticed the elderly woman coming down the stairs holding the hand of no other than little Tonya. She had the most beautiful dress on as well and a smile that would have lit up any room. When she spotted Susan she released the hand of the elderly woman and raced to Susan's side and hugged her with all of her might. Jacob walked over and pulled another chair from the table and said, "May I help you to your seat young lady?"

Tonya, a little embarrassed and never having such treatment before, climbed up and sat quietly on her chair there next to Susan and turned her head and smiled again. Susan could tell that just for a moment she had to feel like a princess. One by one all of the servants came into the room and sat down at the table along with Tonya, Susan and Jacob. It was clear to Susan that what Jacob had told her about everyone sharing equally was true. They all joined hands around the table and Jacob said the prayer as they all bowed their heads and prayed along. When he was finished he looked up at Susan and explained to her that no one here was servant to another, everyone had their role to play and in doing so they all lived happily together. Susan found it hard to believe in these times that this was at all possible, but also felt very honored to be in the presence of such wonderful, caring people.

Shortly after dinner everyone scampered off doing his or her own little chores. It was then that Jacob told Susan that she and Tonya were welcome to stay as long as they wished, but by doing so they too would have to share in on the chores around the plantation. She thanked him kindly, but in the back of her mind she was hoping that she wasn't going to be here that long. The only question she had in her mind now was what she was doing here at all and how long it would be before she served her purpose and returned home with the others.

The days turned to weeks and the weeks to months as Susan settled into her new way of life and found it to be much harder adjusting than she thought. She forgot how easy life was where she had come from, but in some small way learned to enjoy the simple things much more. She had asked Jacob if she could school all the children who lived on the plantation and he thought it to be a wonderful idea, not only to teach the children but also to teach everyone to read who lived there. No one who lived on the plantation had an education of any kind, other than Susan. Not even Jacob had learned to read much more than enough to get him through a letter and then some of the words were more than he could understand or pronounce. To look at him you would have thought he was highly educated because of his manners and appearance, but it was just that he had been taught by his father to be the gentleman he was. She knew without a doubt his father was a very caring man by all the things she had heard about him. Not only from Jacob, but also from everyone whom he had helped here at the plantation. They all knew that their lives would have been very different if it had not been for his dreams for them all to be free someday. It was also clear to her that they all felt the same about Jacob.

As the months turned to years and the seasons changed many times, Tonya was always right there at Susan's side, not only doing her own chores but helping her with schooling all the others. Tonya was now twelve years old and this meant Susan had been here six full years and she had lost total track of time. She often thought about all of those she loved and had left behind, but it made it easier for her to accept, realizing she had no power over her fate.

Jacob came to Susan one night and asked, "Susan, I need to know if you would do me a very important favor?"

Knowing that he was a very honorable man and would never ask her to do something wrong, she replied, "After all you have done for not only Tonya and myself, but all of the others, how could I ever say no to something important to you?"

Jacob smiled and said, "I thank you for that, my dear Susan, you have been more of a gift to us here than we have been of help to you. What I ask is for the others; I need a will to be drawn up so I will be able to make sure the others get what they have been promised if something would ever happen to me. My father had these hopes and dreams of freedom for all, not only those who lived here but throughout the world, and he hadn't been much farther than the harbors to bring the workers home."

Susan sat and listened to his memories of his father and when he was finished she asked, "So what is it exactly that you wish for me to do, Jacob?"

Jacob answered, "I want you to draw up the will nice and proper, naming all of the families here at the plantation to receive a fair share of the land when I have passed. So no man can come along and strip them from what is rightfully theirs."

Susan agreed to do so and in a few days the paper work was complete. Jacob asked her to travel to the next town so the papers could be properly filed. On the way to town, Jacob told her he had been feeling ill for some time, long before she had come to the plantation and as time had passed he could tell that he was getting worse and thought soon, just like his father, he would pass. Susan demanded to know what was wrong with him and wanted to know if there was anything that could be done to help him. He explained to her, there was nothing anyone could do, his father and his father before him all seemed to have the same symptoms as time went on and they all lived to about the same age before becoming ill. He explained how he had watched the way his father passed and how weak he became at the end and how now he was following in those same footsteps. She knew what was wrong with him by the symptoms that he had explained about himself and his father as well. It was cancer. She also knew in these times there was nothing anyone would be able to do to save him.

Fisherman's Fog / 87

Susan sat quietly as the wagon rolled on thinking of what to say next and then asked, "How long do you think you have?"

Jacob, never turning his head or showing any sign of fear said, "A few months at the most. That's why it is important that we get this done now before it is too late."

Now she understood why this was all so important and why it had to be done now and properly. All of those families back at the plantation had placed all of their hopes, dreams and trust in this man and his beloved father.

When they arrived in the city Jacob made his way off to file his paper work and then they stayed the night at the local hotel. This was quite the treat for both of them to see people, other than the people who lived back at the plantation. They enjoyed their dinner and said good night and made their way off to their rooms for the night. When the morning came they loaded up and set out on the long road back to the plantation. Just as it was when they were going, they had to stop and spend one night along the road, making camp along the way. They sat quietly at the fireside and watched as the flames danced like magic fingers in the air. Then before they said goodnight, Susan told him more about where she was from and all the things that were different where she had come from. These stories always brought comfort to Jacob, not only knowing that the world would survive all the hatred, but also there was promise and hope in mankind after all. He lay on his blanket and with a smile on his face, drifted off to sleep. Susan just knew after all she had told him that he had to have all kinds of dreams about the future and this helped her sleep as well.

When the morning came they set off to finish their journey back to the plantation. After traveling most of the day they could see it in the distance as they came through the trees, just as Susan had the first time she came here. The only thing was they could now see smoke, not a lot, but it was clear there had been trouble while they were away. As they arrived in the wagon a few of the men came running out to meet them. They were told how many men had come to burn them out and how they had fought them off once again. Jacob was concerned if there were any loss of life at the plantation, because he knew how hard it was on the families there.

He was told that thirty of the men who attacked had been killed and four from the plantation. This broke Jacob's and Susan's hearts to hear the news, but they knew all they could do now was try to comfort those who had lost family and try to prepare for any further attacks that may come their way.

For the next several weeks things were not the same at the plantation; it always took a while after those attacks for things to return to normal. In the families who had lost their men, the eldest son would step up and take chores where his father left off and all the other families would help out where they could. They could hear the war that had been overtaking the south rumbling in the distance, but it only seemed to make it to the plantation in small raids like the last one that had happened. There had also been rumors that the war was close to an end, but all of this seemed so far away from their world except for when it happened there. For now things were peaceful once again.

Slowly Jacob slipped into his illness, growing weaker by the day, being overtaken by the cancer that was racing through his body. It was clear to Susan that he wasn't going to make it much longer; The only question was how long he could hang on. She could see by the look in his eyes that he was in a great deal of pain and there was nothing she could do to help him. This caused her heartache as well. Tonya had grown to look at him as a father and often sat by his bedside and read to him. He was so grateful that Susan had taught them all how to read, because the stories seemed to take him to another place, away from his pain.

It was one week later that Jacob passed in his sleep while Susan sat quietly holding his hand so he would not be alone. She promised him that she would stay as long as she could and help the others, but she knew she had no idea how long that would be. Jacob was buried on the highest hill on the plantation next to his father and mother, in a place that seemed to be centered in the middle of all of the land there. Everyone gathered around the hill and one by one as they passed and said goodbye just as they had each day as they passed the house where Mr. Abernathy was sitting on the porch as they returned from the fields.

For the next several months, small battles of the war passed through doing little damage and they were able to help those who needed help and fight off those who were looking to cause damage. Susan held off on following through with the terms of Jacob's will, because she knew the war would end soon and she could follow through with it then. She knew then and only then it would have a chance of fulfilling his dreams.

As the next few months passed the rumbling of canons and gunfire became more distant and then suddenly stopped completely. It was only a matter of days before word reached the plantation by way of a soldier on his way back home that the war had indeed ended. The south had surrendered and the war was finally over. Now maybe the killing would stop, Susan hoped. It was then that she decided she would wait one month and then she would take the will to have the land divided and given to those who lived on the plantation as Jacob had requested.

One month later Susan found herself standing in the offices of the land commissioner with the request in her hand, along with the names of each head of household that lived on the plantation. One at a time they were granted a fair share of the ground and the homes they had lived in for so long. There was a surprise she did not expect though and she wasn't sure that she understood how it was placed there without her knowledge. She had been the one to write this all out, she didn't understand how she could have missed this. It was then clear to her that when Jacob took the papers in to be filed he added this part himself while she was waiting at the hotel and then he had it stamped to certify the change that was made. The change stated that Susan received the ownership and equal share of the ground around the big white house. It then states clearly, when and if she ever left the home and moved away, or in her passing, Tonya was to gain ownership at that time. You could have knocked her over with a feather. She had no idea when she taught Jacob how to read and write properly that he would do such a caring, wonderful thing.

Susan returned to the plantation and she and Tonya lived in the big house and continued to do what they were able to for all of the others who lived on the land. Tonya was now teaching the children and Susan was caring for the ill and those injured working in the fields. It was clear by those who came across the plantation in passing, just because the war was over, discrimination was far from over. She knew from history it would take many years before things would change. The one thing they had going for them was they had grown to be a village of their own, pretty much independent from the rest of the world.

The seasons changed as the years passed and the winters there never seemed to be too harsh. For some reason, this year seemed different than most. Susan found herself caring for more and more of the people of their little village because of pneumonia, many of which did not survive the winter. Susan, now an old woman herself, had been working day and night without rest until it took its toll on her as well.

Now she found herself laid up in bed with pneumonia as all of the women rushed to her side.

Susan continued to grow weaker as the days passed and she knew she was not going to pull through this, she had seen it happen too many times before to the others she had been treating. Tonya walked over and fastened the necklace her mother had given her around Susan's neck as she sat by her bedside late one night and read to her from the Bible. Her reading always brought Susan comfort. Not only to listen to the gospel, but to hear the words flow from the mouth of Tonya so clearly and without doubt. Images of finding this little angel so long ago fluttered through her mind and a smile came to her face. Tonya stopped reading and noticed the smile on her face and this brought comfort to her as well. After all, she was the closest thing Tonya had to a mother since that horrible day in the woods. It was then that she noticed the smile never changed and jumped to Susan's side; she was no longer breathing and had gently passed into the night. Tonya closed the book and kissed her on her forehead and wished her a pleasant journey as tears streamed down her face.

The next thing Susan knew she was once again standing in the den of the old estate. The receiver of the phone was still swinging as if she had just dropped it and Rex was standing there looking at her as if he knew she would return. She looked down at herself and noticed her clothes were the same as before she left. She walked over to a mirror that was hanging on the wall and began looking at herself wondering after all of these years how she could look as young as she was when she had left. It was as if she hadn't left at all, but how could this be possible, she thought? She had lived an entire lifetime and seen so many things, but it was as if not a moment was lost and time stood still. She began thinking maybe this didn't happen at all, maybe she had passed out and this had all been a dream.

Just then she heard the rattling of keys as if someone else had made their way into the old estate and when she turned to the door of the den there stood Norman, Sara and Robert, looking at her as if they were surprised that she would be there alone with Rex. After all, they knew how much this old estate, and Rex, gave her the creeps. Susan began telling them all what had happened with the phone and about what she thought had to be a dream. It was then that she realized there was something around her neck. It was the broach that Tonya had given to her and as she held it into her hand she knew then this was not a dream at all. This was the only proof she had that she had spent a lifetime in this very special place.

Not able to fly, Rex turned and ran off hopping from side to side, making a sound as if he were laughing. They could only imagine where he might be off to next.

The Gathering

It was a cool March morning when the phone began to ring at Jim's house. When he answered, it was no other than his old friend Red on the other end. He was very surprised to hear from him because it had been a while since they had last talked. Sometimes it seemed the only time they ever saw each other was when the fishing trip rolled around each year and they headed up north. The lake would always hold a special place in their hearts after entering the fog that day so long ago. It was the adventure of a lifetime and nothing could ever take that away from them.

When Jim realized it was Red, he shouted, "Hey, old man what you up to? It's not like you to drop a dime and spend time on the phone."

Red laughed and replied, "You are right my old friend, I hate these damned phones, always have."

Jim laughed out loud and asked, "I know something is going on or you wouldn't be calling. It's good to hear from you but what's wrong?"

Red paused for a second and then replied, "I don't know what it is, but something has been beckoning me to go to the old estate with the cobble stone rooms, you know Norman and Sara's place."

Jim, without hesitation replied, "Well, how fast can you be ready?"

Red answered, "I will be ready to go when you get here."

Jim knew the conversation was over when he heard the word "later" come from Red's mouth. He always ended his calls that way and then quickly hung up as if the phone company was not going to get another penny of his money. He always liked the simple things in life and a phone wasn't one of those things he needed. Hell, he lived for years without electricity and running water and was perfectly happy.

Jim gathered a few things and kissed his wife Nancy goodbye, and told her that he would get back as soon as he was able. She told him to be careful and to let her know what was going on whenever he got a chance to call. He promised to keep her informed and out the door he ran, jumped into the car drove away. As he did she stood and watched as the car disappeared around the corner and was gone from sight. She couldn't help but worry about what those two would get themselves into next. She knew they had to do what they had to do, simply because they were men.

Jim spent the next hour driving to Red's house out in the woods in the middle of nowhere. It was hard to see the house from the road even as you drove past his place. Many trees surrounded the house and even the driveway was well hidden, the trees created the appearance of a tunnel as you drove through them, because they connected together overhead. As he pulled through the trees he could see Red standing, waiting patiently as if he had heard him coming.

As the car came to a stop Red jumped inside and said, "Thanks for coming."

Jim smiled and said, "You know me Red, I am always up for another adventure. Only thing is did you ever think maybe one of these days we may not make it back?"

Red smiled and said, "I have faith the Lord will only take us where we are meant to be and only see what we are meant to see. If we are not meant to return then we will not."

Jim turned around in the driveway and thought to himself how Red was right and after experiencing what they had in the past they could only have faith in their destination. He couldn't help but notice Red had cut his hair short and no longer had the ponytail in the back. He had cleaned up quite well and was looking better and healthier than he had in years. Jim wasn't quite sure what was going on but he knew it was good to see him doing well.

They had a long drive ahead of them leaving Southern Illinois and heading to the coast up North East where the old estate was located. They also knew the weather up in those parts could be a little unpredictable as well, and they hadn't taken the time to check that at all. Not that the weather would have ever been enough to stop these two from doing something, they would have simply considered it to be another challenge or detour in life. Fortunately for them the roads were clear all the way to the old estate. About two hours before they arrived they stopped to call ahead to let Norman know they were on their way. He was surprised, but also happy to hear from them, because it had been a few years since they had spoken or seen one another. He was looking forward to catching up on what has been going on in their lives and hear what might possess them to drive this far this time of year.

As Jim pulled the car into the drive of the old estate the gates were open as if to welcome them inside and as he looked out the rear view mirror he noticed the gates closing slowly behind him. He couldn't help but think how wonderful it must be to have such privacy from the rest of the world. He lived in a small brick home across from the city park where life never seemed to slow. Even in the wee hours of the morning people were walking the asphalt path around the park to get exercise. Privacy was never an option, you couldn't even sit out on the steps and read the paper without feeling as if everyone was watching you.

They made their way up and around the long driveway and to the rear of the old estate where they found Norman, Sara, Robert and Susan waiting patiently, wondering what it might have been that drove these two adventurous souls to make the trip this time of year. It was rather unseasonably warmer than normal there this time of year, but there was still quite a chill in the air for the old boys from Southern Illinois. Norman invited them inside and as they made their way into the kitchen one by one, they sat at the old wooden table fastened to the floor.

Once they all were seated, Sara poured everyone a hot cup of her special tea in the cups that she had placed before them. As she poured the tea Norman asked, "Well my old friends, what has brought us the pleasure of this visit?"

Red sipped his tea and placed it back upon the table with a soothing sound of "Ahhh" and answered, "Well, Norman I am not sure. I had this overwhelming feeling that I was being beckoned to come here. I do not have the answer as to why, but I always trust my instincts as direction from the Lord."

Jim spoke up and said, "When he called me and told me what he was feeling I wouldn't have missed the trip for the world. You just never know what is going to happen next around here."

They all laughed and agreed that was so very true. Ever since Red returned through the door in the cobblestone room the first time, things have never been the same. They had all experienced adventures one at a time, each seeing something different and returning to share that with the others. Something at first they seemed to fear, but now wouldn't have changed for the world.

As they sat and talked about all the adventures, they heard a loud cawing sound coming from the doorway that exited the kitchen and there stood old Rex. He was ruffling his old black feathers as if he were happy to see they were all there together. Norman couldn't help but feel that somehow, someway Rex had something to do with all of them being in one place at one time. Rex simply stood there watching them turning his head from side to side as he always did, as if he were listening to every word that someone might say. Or could it be that he could hear things they could not.

As they all sat there at the table, Norman glanced out the window and couldn't help but notice a thick fog was starting to settle around the house. They all jumped to the windows in surprise and stood and watched as the fog continued to thicken right before their eyes. It sent cold chills down their spines as they stood there peering out the window and then heard the eerie laugh that could only be coming from Rex as he scampered off into another room. Soon the fog started seeping slowly though every crack and air space that could be found in the old estate, and slowly thickened inside as well. It was only a matter of moments and they couldn't see a thing, not even their own hands in front of their faces. They could feel the cool dampness of the fog as it engulfed each and every one of them. Norman called out for Sara and she was right beside him as he pulled her into his arms and held her tight. He could feel her trembling, and he reached to feel Robert and Susan as well, as they spoke out. Jim and Red had seen this before and knew what it would mean, it was the same fog they had seen on the lake that day and then it had lasted for what seemed to be hours.

Red spoke out in his pirate voice and said, "Looks like times a be changing mates, looks like times a be changing."

Jim replied, "I think it best if we all sit down and wait this out, we have no idea how long this fog will last. The last time we found ourselves in this boat, we were literally in a boat at the time and it took several hours for it to lift."

They could hear the shuffling of movement as they all bent down to sit on the floor beside the windows, after an hour or more, Norman felt what seemed to be the spray of water as it touched his face. He thought to himself how could this be, they never left the house and the windows were protecting them from the outside? Soon he would realize what it was that caused him and the others to feel the cold spray of water that invaded their space. Then he could hear what sounded as if it were water rushing past and the clatter of other voices coming closer and closer all the time.

Slowly the fog began to thin as they waited patiently. Soon they were able to faintly see one another and stood back to their feet. They grasped a railing along their side where the windows once were, as the wind rushed past their faces with the scent of saltwater in the air. As quickly as the fog had come it disappeared as well, leaving them all standing at the railing of what appeared to be a cruise ship. Now they were all a little confused about how they could have all left the house and still be together as they all stood there looking around.

A young gentleman wearing a white jacket and holding what seemed to be a small computer devise in his hand came whisking past, and Red reached out and grabbed him by his arm. As he turned and looked into Red's eyes, Red said, "Excuse me, we are a little disoriented and confused, is there some way you can tell us where we are and where our rooms are?" Hell, he was just hoping they had a room at all at this point.

The gentleman smiled and asked him for his name and then punched it into the devise he was holding in his hand and replied, "Yes Sir, you are on the maiden voyage

Fisherman's Fog / 99

of the Angelina, you are in room Sixteen C, with another gentleman named Jim."

Red knew him and then one by one the others asked the same question, finding out where their rooms were all located next to each other. No reservations, on a ship they could only wonder what their purpose might be. They got together and made sure all their rooms were located to their liking inside of each room. Clothes were laid out across the beds as if they were to go down to dinner. Norman was quick to notice not only the time had changed on them late, but so had the date as well. They were now six months into the future. As they returned to the other's rooms to share what they discovered, they too were a little confused as to what would happen. They had all one by one gone back into the past, but up to this point no one had ever jumped into the future. Now the question in their minds was if this was true then why? Robert had a notion that only Rex knew the answer to that one and he was sure they would all find out soon enough why they were here.

They all agreed to shower and dress for dinner and meet again in one hour. Red wasn't much into the idea of getting all duded up just to eat, but he agreed just the same. Hell, he was quite hungry at this point after making the long road trip and then coming through the fog. It looked like if he was going to get something to eat he was going to have to go along with the plan as he scampered back to his room mumbling in discontent all the way. Jim couldn't help but laugh knowing how much this was going to kill Red to get all dressed up. When they opened their luggage it looked as if they had planed well for this very sort of thing. Even Red had all the clothes that he needed and most of them were things he would have never worn.

In one hour they all met out in the hallway in front of their rooms, dressed for dinner and ready to go. Red tailed slowly behind and it was easy to tell he was not comfortable at all with this whole arrangement. As they made their way down to the dining room, they passed two men in the corridor and the one gentleman looked at Red and Jim as if he were a little uncomfortable. As they made eye contact with one another it was clear to see that the gentlemen were of Middle Eastern descent, and as they passed, they spoke to each other with the language to match. As Red continued down the corridor, he turned his head and looked back at the two gentlemen and one of them had done the same and was looking back at him.

When they arrived into the dining room, the room was most elegant and there was enough food placed out for twice as many people as were present on the ship. Robert laughed and said, "Can you imagine the food that is wasted on a ship like this each day? Enough to feed a lot of hungry people around the world I bet."

Susan replied, "Only you would think of a thing like that in a time like this, just try to not make a scene please."

Norman turned to the group and said, "This table is large enough to accommodate all of us, would that be alright with everyone?"

Red spouted, "Looks good to me, besides the longer we walk around in here the more we bring attention to ourselves."

Jim knew this was not the sort of thing Red would enjoy and joined in, "Red, just try to make the best of it, you know we wouldn't be here if there wasn't a very good reason."

Red, still not happy, grunted, "Yeah, you're right but that doesn't mean I have to like it just the same. Let's just find out what we are doing here and find the way out."

Jim answered, "Well, old buddy I have a feeling that is not going to be as easy to do as you think."

The food was not being served it was all placed out to help yourself to whatever you may want. Norman and Jim weren't too comfortable about that, because they were both germophobic and could only imagine what could be present on food that had been lying out. They were both very hungry just the same, and managed to find a few things they were comfortable eating. They were all very hungry at this point and glad to just be eating something and able to get a little better bearing on where they were. They all returned to the table and joined hands and prayed together giving thanks for all they had been given and shown through their lives. One by one they took turns verbally giving thanks for something that happened in their lives this day. Then they quietly sat and ate their food they had chosen.

A few moments into the meal, two men walked into the dining room and fired shots into the air with what seemed to be automatic weapons. They were the same two men Red and Jim had passed in the corridor. Then two of the men cleaning off the tables had towels over their arms, and exposed their weapons as well as shots rang out once again.

The man who had looked back at Red in the corridor shouted, "Everyone stay seated, we are taking over this ship and anyone who moves will be shot and killed without question."

Then the second man they had passed in the corridor stated, "We have ten men on this ship with automatic weapons and we have placed five bombs in a place that has been assigned to them. This ship will explode and sink to the bottom of the ocean in two hours.

If you have anything to say to your so-called God, I suggest that you do that now."

Norman slowly rose to his feet and asked, "Why in the world would you want to do this to innocent people?"

The man answered, "No one is innocent, the world and our people are suffering and you chose to look the other way, or have sided with our enemies."

In response Norman replied, "We have done nothing to you and your people, we are but simple people and we mean you no harm."

The man, becoming frustrated with the continuing conversation, shouted, "This is a statement to show no matter where you are and how safe you feel you will not be, as long as we do not live in peace nor will the rest of the world."

Norman sat back down before frustrating the men any more than he had already. It was clear there would be no reasoning with these men and they had no idea at all where the other six men might be at this time. As they all sat there at the table the only thing they knew for sure was, they had two hours to do something if it were going to happen.

Red leaned forward and quietly said, "I am not much for sitting and dying, especially not this way. We are going to have to do something before it is too late."

They all didn't want to think this could really be happening at all but it was, as they all nodded their heads to show they agreed something would have to be done and soon. Just then the man who seemed to be in charge ordered the two men cleaning off the tables to go to the kitchen and bring back everyone working there. The two men moved without question, it didn't seem to bother them to know that in two hours they would be dying as well.

Now that there were only two men left in the room, Red leaned forward once again and whispered, "We need a diversion of some sort to get one of the men with their weapons to come close enough to over-take him."

Norman leaned toward Robert and whispered, "Robert, lean over and fall out of your chair and into the floor."

Robert frowned and replied, "Why?"

Norman answered, "You seem to be good at falling through and over stuff you should be good at that sort of thing by now."

Robert, not sure how to take that, replied, "This is no time to be funny Norman, this is serious stuff here, someone could get killed."

Norman shook his head in confusion and said, "I've got news for you Robert, if we don't do something quick we are all going to die."

Robert looked toward Red and Jim and they both nodded in agreement that he should do as Norman had asked. Robert picked up his napkin and wiped his mouth, as if it were going to matter that he displayed manners even in a time like this. Robert then dropped his napkin to the floor and then reached over as to pick it up and the chair flipped on its side, and Robert went with it with a thud. As he did, the man standing the closest came running over to see what the commotion was all about and just as he reached the table, Jim smashed his drinking glass into the man's face and he fell to the floor. Red instantly ripped the gun from his hand, turned and shot the second man three times in the chest, driving him backward and killing him instantly. Then he turned and shot the man on the floor as well. This seemed to upset the ladies very much, but Norman did his best to explain to them if they lived they would do everything they could to kill them all and accomplish their mission. No one wanted anyone to die, but there were many other lives at stake and they would all be lost if something wasn't done.

Along side of the man lying next to their table was a briefcase he had dropped when falling to the floor. Robert reached over and carefully examined it for any kind of trigger device and then flipped it open, exposing the plastic explosives and timer device inside. Realizing it was simple wiring and did not have a trigger device to set it off if tampered with, so he pulled the wires free to separate the timer and the explosives. Then he turned and said, "We need to find the rest of these cases and fast."

Red, knowing the shots would be heard and others would be coming soon, shouted, "Everyone quickly go back to your rooms and lock yourselves inside where you will be safe for now. Move as quickly and as quietly as possible and search your cabins for cases like the one we found here with this man. If you find one place a towel on the doorknob outside your room and we will see it."

Red asked Norman to help Sara and Susan back to their rooms and then meet him, Jim and Robert back at the railing where they had arrived. Norman picked up the automatic weapon from the second man and escorted Sara and Susan out of the dining room and down the corridor to their rooms, telling them to stay together and search the rooms for a case and he would be back soon. Sara wasn't too happy about being separated at this time, but she knew this had to be done if they were going to save all of these people. She kissed him goodbye and he scampered off back to meet the others.

When Norman got back at the railing where they had arrived Red, Robert and Jim were waiting as planned. They knew there were eight terrorists left on the ship and they would have to deal with them first or others would be killed. They agreed to split up in groups of two, that way each group had a weapon to defend themselves if needed.

Red said, "Norman, you and Robert head back to the dining room. Soon the other two men will be coming back with all the workers from the kitchen. You should be able to get the drop on them if they did not hear the shots."

Norman replied, "They shouldn't be too concerned with the shots, I wouldn't think, after all they came in shooting and they will be expecting anyone who resists to be shot to maintain control."

Jim replied, "Norman old friend, I hope you are right, you and Robert keep your heads down and we will meet back here in one hour."

Norman and Robert nodded their heads and ran off in the direction of the dining room, hoping to get back there before the men returned with the workers from the kitchen. As they came down the corridor to the dining room, a group of people came around the corner followed by the two men with their guns pointed at their backs. Norman and Robert stepped into an open door and pushed it almost closed so they could still see, they looked at each other hoping the two men hadn't seen them as they came around the corner. One of the men with the guns was short and the other was tall. Norman made a gesture with his hands indicating that he would take out the tall man and for Robert to take the short one down as well. Robert nodded to show he understood as they sat patiently waiting for everyone to pass the doorway. Just as the two men passed, Norman ripped the door open and clubbed the tall man over the head with the butt of the rifle. As the second man turned to respond, Robert took him down with the force of a linebacker in a football game, he never knew what hit him as Norman struck him with the butt of the gun as well.

Robert scampered back into the room and removed the cords from all of the lamps. He returned to tie the men up good and tight leaving the men from the kitchen to watch over them with one of the guns. Now both Norman and Robert had rifles. Norman just hoped Robert didn't accidentally shoot him with the damn thing.

Norman turned to Robert and said, "Four down and six to go, got any ideas where to look next?"

Robert replied, "If I were taking over this ship I would have a couple of men in the bridge and a couple more in the engine room."

Norman answered, " Good thinking, I am sure Jim and Red are making their way to the bridge as we speak, so let's make our way down to the engine room, but keep your eyes open. We don't want to get caught off guard."

Meanwhile Norman was correct, Red and Jim had made their way to the bridge. Jim, peeking through the side of the window, could clearly see there were two men inside with rifles and what looked like grenades strapped to their sides. He crawled back away from the door and whispered to Red, "Looks like we have a problem. There are two with rifles and grenades on their belts, and I heard one of the men telling the Captain to shut the engines down."

Red looked at Jim and said, "So, what's the problem?"

Jim answered, "Hell, man doesn't anything ever get to you? There are two men with automatic weapons and explosives in that room and we only have one gun, and you have that. Don't expect me to not be worried about those odds."

Red smiled and said, "Have a little faith brother, we wouldn't be here now if we were not meant to be. Stop thinking about all of that and let's come up with a plan."

Jim shook his head and said, "You are right my friend, there are a lot of people to save here. I have all the faith in the world the Lord will guide us through this as he has so many other things."

They talked it over and decided to make a noise in the corridor and when one of the men came to check it out they would be waiting for him. Jim took the fire extinguisher down from the wall and placed it on the floor just a few feet down from the room where they were hiding. He pulled the pin and then the trigger on the extinguisher and then jammed the pin back in to keep it flowing. As the loud

Fisherman's Fog / 107

hissing noise from the extinguisher sprayed out, the fog shot past the window of the bridge.

One of the men shouted, "Go see what's going on out there!"

As the second man made his way out into the hallway into the fog, Red stepped out of the room and clubbed him across the back of the neck with the rifle he was carrying. The man dropped like a sack of potatoes, as Jim grabbed his gun before it hit the ground. Still conscious, he grabbed for one of the grenades from his side and pulled the pin. But before he could release the trigger, Jim grabbed his hand and squeezed tight placing the pin back into place as the man slipped off into unconsciousness. Red clubbed him a couple of times for good measure and then slithered over to the bridge door on his belly and slowly pulled the door open from below. As the door reached the halfway open mark it squeaked ever so slightly and the man inside with the gun turned to see who it was. But it was too late. Red had his sites on him and popped him twice with two short bursts of fire. The Captain fell to the floor as Red climbed to his feet as he shouted, "Ahoy Captain, we are here to help and we are taking this ship back. Now get those engines fired back up and get us moving!"

Norman and Robert were down below the decks and did not hear the shots, but were about to close in on the engine room. They had heard the engines stop and now they heard them firing back up again, to them that could only be a good sign that Red and Jim had made their way to the bridge and had taken control of the ship. As they stood with their backs pressed up against the wall outside the engine room, they heard several men inside talking, one was telling the other to go find out why the engines were starting back up and see if there was a problem. As he stepped out into the hallway Norman took him down with a ripple of shots across his chest just as Robert dove across the entrance of the engine room, eyes searching for the other man. A rain of gunfire rang out and it was not from his weapon and he returned fire, dropping the man in his tracks as his gun sprayed bullets across the ceiling of the engine room. Then there was only the sound of the engines running again. Norman looked down to his watch and noticed that it had been fifty minutes since they left Jim and Red along the railing. They had agreed to meet back there in one hour if they were still alive and motioned to his arm to let Robert know it was time to return as they shot down the corridor heading back to the railing.

When they arrived, Jim and Red were there waiting and Red mumbled, "You're late, and we had just about given up on you two."

Kneeling down along the railing Robert replied, "We have been a little too busy trying to save our lives to worry about the time."

Red answered, "Time is everything here Robert, we only have another hour to clean up this mess and find the other four bombs."

Norman said, "We got the two men from the kitchen and then two more from the engine room, that makes six."

Jim replied, "Eight, we got two more from the bridge, that means there are two left, any ideas?"

Red answered, "Yes, we need to get to the pool area of the ship. I noticed a large gathering of people standing out there on the deck while on the bridge. I have a sneaky feeling they are holding everyone else there. Let's make this quick. We are running out of time."

Quickly, the four of them ran to the other end of the ship to discover Red's thoughts were correct. The two men remaining were making everyone with cell phones call their loved ones to tell them what was going to happen. The terrorists wanted to leave no doubt in the minds of the world what they were doing here and why. This way they felt they could create panic throughout the world and no one would ever feel safe again. Red motioned with the barrel of the gun that they all needed to circle around behind them and get them from behind. When they were all in position and timing was right, Red bolted out and began firing until his clip was empty. The passengers all fell to the floor and took cover staying clear of any shots that were being fired, as the two men fell lifeless to the deck and never saw it coming.

Red shouted, "It's all right, everyone can get back to their feet, we have over taken all of the terrorists and now we must all start looking for the briefcase bombs they have brought aboard the ship."

As one of the gentleman passengers rose to his feet he shouted, "I watched one of the men slide a briefcase under one of the tables to your left."

Jim turned in search of the table the man had spoken of and sure enough there it was. Knowing there were no trigger devises he flipped it open and pulled the wires loose from the explosives once again. Then turned and said, "There are only three bombs left on the ship according to one of the men, we must all spread out and search for the three remaining cases that look like this one."

Robert replied, "Maybe someone should prepare the life boats just in case we do not find them all in time."

Another gentleman spoke out, "The life boats have been lost, I saw one of the men earlier cutting them loose and dropping them overboard."

Red answered, "More the reason we must find these bombs before it is too late, it's our only chance to save everyone here. Norman, you and Robert go back to the rooms to get Sara and Susan and start the search on the bridge and upper decks."

Robert and Norman turned and were off like a flash of light heading back to the room to let Sara and Susan know what was going on and to help them search for the three remaining bombs. When they arrived at the room, the ladies were very happy to see that they were both still alive and neither of them had been injured. Together they all made their way to the bridge and began their search for the cases. One by one, they combed every nook and cranny until Susan spotted something stashed behind the control panel of the bridge. She called out for Robert and he bolted to her side because he knew she had found something or she would not have been calling. He could hear the adrenaline racing through her voice as she shouted out his name.

He crawled into the opening and looked inside. Sure enough it was one of the cases, but the opening was too small for him to get through to reach the case. He crawled back out and by then Sara had heard the yelling as well and was standing at Susan's side. Robert looked at the two of them and told them the opening was too small for him to reach the case, one of them would have to go in after it. Sara, without hesitation pushed him aside and shot through the opening, in search of the case. In a matter of only a minute she was sliding back out of the opening handing the case to Robert before coming out. He opened the case just as they had the others and pulled the wires free, disabling it as well.

Robert said, "Well done ladies, two more cases and we are home free. Let's check on the others and see how they are doing."

For thirty minutes or more Norman, Robert, Susan and Sara searched the remainder of the deck for any sign of another case without any more luck. They knew it was time to move on and see if Red and Jim had had any luck searching with the other passengers. They all met up in the corridor that led back to the rooms where they were staying. They had been in search of the rooms where the terrorists had been assigned and their search was successful. They had managed to not only find their rooms they had found one of the cases had been slipped under one of the beds as well. This meant only one case would remain and time was running out fast, there was less than thirty minutes before the timer on the last bomb would reach its deadline.

As they stood in the corridor, Red said, "Well, looks like this is it, if we don't find that last case fast this ship is going down, we only have a few minutes left, does anyone have any suggestions?"

Susan replied, "Didn't you say there were a couple of men down in the engine room?"

Robert replied, "Yes, but we took them both out, what does that have to do with anything?"

Norman said, "She is right, every place we had confronted the terrorists so far is where the bombs were found, we never found a bomb in the engine room before we headed back to meet Red and Jim at the railing."

Red shouted, "Good thinking Susan, now let's all get to the engine room and fast. I only hope we can get there before it's too late."

Together they all scampered to the decks below and to the engine room, spreading out to search for anything that might look remotely like the final case or bomb. The minutes continued to slip by without any sign of hope to find the final case, all of a sudden Susan stumbled across what seemed to be the final case stashed behind the pipes along the wall. She knew she did not have time to spare and yelled out to the others and they all came running to her side. She pulled the case out from behind the pipes and gently laid it down to be opened. Robert stepped in and flipped the two latches and peeled back the lid carefully once again. It was as he reached for the wires the clock stuck zero and the bomb went off with a powerful blast. They were but a split second too late.

They all felt the heat from the blast and saw the flash, but nothing more. The room was now dark and they could see nothing, not even their own hands before their faces once again. They were once again engulfed into the fog that had brought them there in the beginning. For several minutes they all sat motionless and then a voice rang out, "Can anyone hear me?"

It was Norman's voice and Sara replied, "Yes, dear. I am here, are you all right?"

Norman replied, "Yes, I think so but I can not see a thing. Are you all right?"

Red jumped in and shouted, "Yes, we are all right just as we have always been before, but I don't know what has happened to all of those people on the ship. Everyone just sit tight. I am sure when this fog lifts we will get the answers we need."

It was only a few more minutes, and slowly the fog began to lift, now finding themselves at the very window they had left at the old estate. As they climbed to their feet they turned to notice Rex standing tall on top of the edge of the old wooden table behind them. No one knew what to think about this, but they were sure Rex was about to tell them or show them something. It was then Rex raised his feathers and wings as if to fly, as he began to glow with a light so bright it was all they could do to continue to see what was happening. He changed right before their eyes into the most beautiful angel, tall and radiant with blue light, with his arms extending forward toward them. They all stood in total amazement at what Rex truly was and couldn't believe this large scary black bird was something so powerful and beautiful all along and no one ever knew.

For the first time, Rex spoke out and said, "I have taken you all on many journeys and have brought you all together once again. You have been shown the past and lessons to be remembered and chances to right what had gone wrong. Now I have sent you all into the future and you have seen what you must do to stop what is not meant to be. Go forth and right this wrong and use what I have shown you to change the world, in the name of the Lord."

The light slowly dimmed as the angel slowly transformed back to the large black bird that Rex had been known as for so very many years. They were left standing wondering was Rex truly this angel or was the angel simply using Rex to convey his messages? The truth to that would never be known, but they all knew they would never look at him the same after this day, they would never fear him again.

Norman walked over to the phone, picked it up and called his travel agent and requested six tickets for the cruise ship Angelina, a new ship that would be sailing in six months. His tickets were confirmed and all the arrangements were being made by the agent.

After hanging up the phone he turned and said, "Well this should be an easy one for us. We know where we are going and who our enemies are and we also know the locations of all the cases we spent so much time looking for. We will be able to stop it this time because we have all the answers we need."

Red replied, "Well my friends, we have had a lot of questions answered here today and now I know why I was drawn to come back to this old estate once again. I will say my goodbyes and see you all in about six months."

They walked Jim and Red back to the car and they said their goodbyes as Rex stood in the window inside and flared his wings and cawed with all his might as if to say farewell.

William

The air was cool and brisk as the seasons began to change, summer was saying her final goodbye and fall was beginning to show her true colors. Susan was standing out behind the old estate and the wind was blowing through her hair, as she thought about all the things that this year had brought about. Much sadness, but many good times as well, as she stood with a tear in her eyes, but yet a peaceful smile upon her face. Because she knew she was not alone, she was always surrounded by those who loved her and the Lord was always at her side.

As she stood there thinking, Robert came running toward the house, he had been out at the old schoolhouse that had been moved last year. It was a large old schoolhouse that had been moved from the far side of the property, so it could be preserved and restored. The ladies could also use the old structure for quilting and gatherings of sorts. Many treasures of the past had been found in the land around the old schoolhouse through the past year that would date back many years. Some were things that had been lost while the children played in the lot and trees that surrounded the old schoolhouse. Even old arrowheads from the Indians that had been lost long before the schoolhouse was ever built on this site. One of the things that had been found was a smooth rock shaped like a heart, with the names William on one side and Annie on the other. It was found in one of the old desks that had remained in the old schoolhouse and had fallen out when overturned. It seemed to be hidden as if not meant to be found until that moment in time. Both Susan and Norman had held the rock in their hand and wondered what had become of these two lovers of so long ago and what fate life had brought them. Robert was shouting something, but Susan wasn't quite sure what it was he was saying, because the wind was blowing rather briskly toward him and away from her.

As he reached where she was standing he stopped to catch his breath with his hands resting on his knees. He looked up at her and said, "I just heard on the radio, the hurricane has taken a turn and will be heading inland. It will take land a few miles from here sometime tomorrow."

Susan and all the others knew of the hurricane, but first predictions were that she was going to head back out into the deeper waters of the ocean and away from land. It was almost as if the Lord had pushed her in another direction, the only question in her mind now was why? She tried to never question why the Lord did the things he did, because she knew in her heart and soul even if she did not understand, he always had his reasons. Sometimes we did not understand until we were able to see the bigger picture. She walked back into the house and informed Norman and Sara of what was about to happen.

Norman replied, "Everyone stay calm, this old estate has stood here for many years and has seen many hurricanes in the past and is still standing. We will all be safe here, even the old schoolhouse has weathered all of the storms of the past, so do not worry."

He could still see the concern in their eyes but Robert answered, "He is right. As long as we all stick together and baton down the hatches we will be fine here."

Norman couldn't help but laugh, after all Robert there for a moment sounded like an old pirate or something. He thought to himself, all you have to do now Robert is put Rex on your shoulder and you would fit the image just fine.

Robert looked at Norman and said, "What are you smiling about? There is nothing funny about this, this is dangerous stuff."

Norman, still smiling even more so now replied, "Just a silly picture that raced through my mind, nothing to concern yourself about old boy, now let's get to work."

Sara and Susan began closing off all the windows on the east side of the house, that would be the direction from which the hurricane would be approaching with winds of possibly a hundred or more miles per hour when she hit shore. Norman and Robert went out to check the guesthouse and barn to make sure everything was secure and safe. They could tell the winds were starting to build and it wasn't going to take long before the rains would start pounding at them. All they hoped was to finish up and make it back to the house before the rains started to fall.

Norman told Robert to head on over to the old schoolhouse and make sure everything was secured there as well. The sky had begun to darken from the clouds overhead as Robert lit the lamp just inside the door of the schoolhouse. He then raced to make sure all the windows and shutters were all fastened tightly. He then stepped out the door and fastened it behind him making sure it was secure as well. As a light rain began to fall he turned and saw Norman motioning to him to head back to the house, as he was heading in that direction as well.

By the time they both arrived back to the house, conditions had continued to become worse. The sun was beginning to set and the darkness was beginning to set in even faster with the thick dark cloud overhead. Norman turned and noticed several cars heading up the long driveway to the old house. It was family and friends who had heard the news of the hurricane changing direction and they knew this old house would be the safest place for them all to gather. They thought even if things were to go bad, at least they would all be together.

Once inside Norman scampered off upstairs to get out of his wet clothes and into something dry. He no sooner reached the top of the stairs and the lights went out. Sara and Susan had planned ahead for this and had candles and oil lamps lit just in case the winds would knock the lines out. Norman hesitated for a second to regain focus and then continued on his quest for dry clothing. Robert kept a few things at the house as well just in case he had to stay the night and watch the place when they were out of town, so he scampered off into a dark room to change into something dry also. He figured it was going to be a long night.

As the winds continued to gain strength and power, Susan stood at the back of the house and in the distance, deep into the darkness, she could see a glimmer of light flickering ever so lightly. She knew it was in the direction of the old schoolhouse and being the teacher she was, this old building had a special place in her heart. Her first thought was that in the rush of closing everything up, they forgot to shut the oil lamp off before leaving. They did not notice it was still lit because the darkness had not set in yet. She wasn't about to ask Norman or Robert to go back out into the rain, so she slipped off and out the door while she thought no one was looking. But someone was, Sara saw her running out into the darkness and toward the old schoolhouse before she lost sight of her completely.

Sara yelled out, "Norman, Robert come quickly, I think we have a problem."

Both Norman and Robert came running and found Sara standing at the back door yelling for Susan to return. Robert said, "What the Sam Hell is going on?"

Sara turned and said, "I saw Susan run out the door and toward the old schoolhouse but it is too dark to see her. I think I saw the door open on the schoolhouse and there was light on inside."

Robert instantly answered, "The lamp, I left the lamp burning in the old schoolhouse when I locked it up. I didn't even notice it in the rush."

Norman started out the door then looked back and said, "I will go get her and bring her back, everyone else stay put. I don't want to have to go out looking for anyone else in this storm."

Robert pulled Sara back into the door and closed it as Norman disappeared into the darkness in search of Susan. One thing he knew for sure was that Susan was inside and safe from the storm. Then the rain began to pound and the wind blew with a fury, as if it were trying to stop him from reaching the old schoolhouse. He found himself grabbing and clutching at anything he could find, even the blades of grass upon the ground, inching his way toward the old building. It was raining so hard the rain was beginning to blow sideways and he was only a few feet away from the building but could hardly make it out. He knew if he made it to the old schoolhouse they would never make it back now that the hurricane had reached this level.

It was then, when he was pawing at the ground, grasping at every inch of grip he could find, when lightning struck the old building with a flash as if to guide his way. As he reached the door and forced his way inside he found the lamp still burning and Susan was no place to be found. He called out her name several times but there was no answer, she was gone. He had seen this kind of thing now too many times to think it could be anything other than a journey into the unknown for Susan again. He sat down in one of the old desks and knew he would have no choice but to wait out the storm here where it was safe and be there just in case Susan would return.

Little did Norman know he was sitting at the same desk Susan was in when she disappeared, but soon he figured it out as he noticed the shape of the smooth heart shaped rock the two of them had found, burnt there in the top of the desk, with the name William clear for him to see. He couldn't help but wonder where Susan had made off to and if she was all right as he sat there praying for her safe return and the safety of all of those he left behind back at the house. He knew Robert would take care of things back there now all he needed was for this old schoolhouse to hold together until the storm passed or Susan made it back safely.

Susan found herself far from the winds and rain of the hurricane. The sun was shining as she found herself standing at what appeared to be a graveyard of so many years ago. About fifty feet away she noticed a frail old man who looked to be very, very old, digging what appeared to be a hole for someone to be put to rest. She slowly walked over to the old gentleman, careful not to frighten him and said, "Hello, my name is Susan and I was wondering if maybe you could tell me where I am?"

The old man jabbed his shovel into the ground so it would stay there until he retuned and climbed up out of the hole. When he climbed to his feet he dusted off his hands on his old worn trousers and extended it to Susan and said, "My name is William and I am the caretaker here. You are in St. John's cemetery out past the edge of town."

Susan opened her hand and in it was the smooth heart shaped rock and she didn't know how it got there. As she looked at it she couldn't help but ask, "Are you the same William who carved his name in this rock?"

William stood with a look of confusion on his face and stared at the rock and then looked at Susan, as tears started to form in his eyes. He then mumbled, "How can this be true? I lost this rock when I was but a young boy and so in love with my darling Annie."

Susan smiled and handed the rock to William as the tears started to flow freely from his eyes. He rolled the rock gently over in his hand and read the word "Annie", which he had scratched on the rock so many years ago. He then pressed it gently against his lips as if to kiss her once again.

Susan stood silently for a moment and let William take in the memories and then broke her silence as she asked, "William, what ever became of Annie?"

William looked into her eyes and answered, "She became my lovely bride and we had two wonderful children together."

Susan smiled and replied, "Could you tell me more about your lives?"

William looked back down to the rock and then asked, "Would It be all right with you if I kept the rock?"

Susan smiled once again and with tears in her own eyes as well she answered, "Yes, I have a feeling that is why I was sent here."

William slipped the rock carefully into his pocket, now curious as to who she was, asked, "May I be so bold as to ask you who you are and where you came from?"

Susan wiped the tears from her eyes and said, "Well, it's a long story and I am not sure where to begin, but my name is Susan and I believe the Lord has brought me here to see you."

He smiled, then explained that he must finish digging the grave before sunset and then asked her if she would honor him by having a cup of coffee with him when he was finished? Susan nodded her head yes and stood patiently as the old frail frame of a man crawled back into the hole and began digging once again. The handle on the shovel looked as old and weathered as the hands on William as he dug as if he were given the energy to do his job. It was hard for Susan to believe a man who looked to be more than eighty years old was still able to do such a task so effortlessly.

In a matter of only a few minutes the hole was completed and William once again pulled himself up and out of the ground. As he climbed to his feet and dusted the dirt off of his clothes he motioned for Susan to follow him as he walked off out of the graveyard and into the woods nearby. She was a little nervous at first, but knew she would not have been sent here if she was in any danger of any kind, and simply had faith in her mission. As she followed close behind, the light of the sun was slowly dimming as she could see the old wooden shack they were approaching.

William turned to her, shovel still in his hand and said, "It's not much but it is all I have needed for many years now. I will light a lamp inside so we can sit and talk a spell if you don't mind?"

As she stepped up on the porch of the old wooden shack she replied, "I would be most honored to sit and talk with you and share so many memories of your life."

He walked over to the window and picked up the old oil lamp and lit it, setting it in the center of the table, filling the room with light. It was clear to see he didn't need or require many things in life and that he had been alone for some time, leaving her to wonder what had become of Annie and his two children that he had spoken of earlier that evening. She sat down at the table in one of only two old wooden chairs as William lit the fire in the wood-burning stove to heat a pot of coffee. He explained to her most of the time he just drank it cold, but it was special to have a guest. This was something he didn't have that often and a cup of hot coffee would be nice this evening. Susan cringed at how old and dirty the water and pot must be, but wasn't about to spoil this special moment for him.

She looked over in the corner and noticed the small flat bed in which he slept and the bible that lay along side on the floor. She couldn't help but ask, "William, how long have you been living here?"

He answered, "Many, many years now, I have been the caretaker of this graveyard most of my life and have seen many come and go as the years have past."

He walked over to the table where she was sitting and placed a clean china cup on the table in front of her and a tin cup in front of the chair in which he would be sitting. He then poured her a cup of coffee that smelled absolutely divine. All the thoughts of the water escaped her mind, as if it were a magic potion of some sort, even though she knew it was not. As he poured the coffee into her cup he said, "Now it is my turn, who are you and why are you here?"

Susan took a sip from her small china cup and then answered, "As I said before, my name is Susan and I do not know what I am doing here. The last thing I remember was sitting in the old schoolhouse where I had found the smooth rock with yours and Annie's name engraved. There was a hurricane approaching and then there was a large flash of lightning, blinding to the eyes. When my vision cleared I found myself standing in the graveyard where you were digging the hole. I know no more than you, I guess you could say."

He laid the rock gently upon the table and smiled and said, "I guess I could ask for nothing more of you then, but I would like to thank you and the Lord for sending you today."

She replied, "May I ask you what has become of your wife and children?"

He paused for a moment as if to gather his thoughts, then slowly looked up into her eyes and said, "Just as the hurricane has brought you to me, one had taken them from my life as well. More than fifty years ago they were torn from my life and our home was destroyed. They were taken from me then, but yet I remained. I did not understand that at first, but in time it all became quite clear to me."

He then explained how he had always done this job since a young boy and after he had lost his family he saw no reason to rebuild a home only for himself. So he simply moved in to the old caretaker shack to be close to his work. He told her how he was given a gift of being able to touch the casket of those who had left this world and for a brief moment he would hear the last words they wish to say. How some were no more than how grateful they were to leave this world and others, special messages they wish to be conveyed to their loved ones.

Susan sat there in amazement sipping on her china cup of coffee, no longer even caring about the water or the pot it was brewed in. She had so many questions she would like to ask. But was afraid she would spark old memories that may be painful for him. But he could see the curiosity in her eyes.

He smiled and said, "Ask your questions young lady, that is why you are here, to find what you must find and understand why you have found the rock that held my heart. Much like the rock, until you handed it to me, my heart had turned to stone, for so many years I forgot what it was like to feel such love and passion inside. Death has a way of doing that to a man."

With tears in her heart but not in her eyes she asked, "I do not mean to be insensitive, but were you able to hear the last thoughts of those you love as well?"

"Yes, I was. My darling wife told me she would miss me and would wait for me in heaven when my job here was through. My children said they loved me and then their thoughts were gone as well. It wasn't much, but enough to let me know they had gone on to a better place and were now with our Lord," he answered.

He told her how he had dug each of their graves with his own hands as he had each and every soul buried in the graveyard. He didn't want someone else to be the one to place them there. How this gave him his chance to say his final goodbyes and to touch their caskets as he had so many before.

They sat there at the table until the wee hours of the night talking about all the people's lives he had touched and messages he had delivered. How some of the people simply looked at him as if he were some kind of nut and others clearly understood the message he was to deliver. In many cases it was something only the deceased and the one to receive the message would understand. Sometimes it was to help them find what they need to find or to know to beware of who would cause them harm if not careful. Mostly they were just goodbyes and promises to be waiting to see them again. He told her of one man who had cheated people all of his life and hid the money away so no one would ever find it, but yet his last request was to retrieve the money and return it all to those he had cheated. Then told about another man who had killed a man and buried him to never be found and his family never knew what had happened to him, they simply thought he had run off and left them all. His wish was for the body to be found and bring closure to the family he had wronged.

He then reached out and took Susan's hand, rolled it over and placed ten silver dollars in her hand and said, "You will need this before you go from here."

She didn't know what to say other than she did not want his money, but then he explained there would be things she would need and her money would not be accepted or understood here and now. She knew in her heart this was true and told him somehow she would repay him for his kindness. He then told her it was not necessary, she had already given him more than she could ever know.

Susan found this all so interesting, but as the night drifted on sometime during the night, she had laid her head down on her arm and slipped off to sleep. When she opened her eyes in the light of the morning, the sun beginning to rise, William was tucked neatly in his bed appearing to be sound asleep. She sat there for some time before she realized, William had slipped off during the night and had left this world. Little did she know the grave she had interrupted him from digging last night was his own. The tears flowed freely from her eyes and she said a gentle prayer and asked the Lord to take him to his family. She knew then and there what her purpose was for coming there that night, it was so he would not be alone and he could share his last moments with someone who cared.

She notified the people at the church nearby that he had passed during the night and then made her way into town to find a place to stay. She found a nice place nearby with rooms to sleep, more what we call today a bed and breakfast. The kind old woman told her it would be two dollars in advance and one dollar a day for meals. She reached into her pocket and handed the woman three of the silver dollars William had given her the night before. Now she understood why he had given them to her, but still unclear as to why so much. Little did she know it would be because she had to remain at this home for three days, totaling nine silver dollars.

On the third day, William was to be placed in the ground and a service for him was to be conducted at the graveyard for all to come. When she arrived, there was no one there except the minister and the new caretaker who had been hired. She thought how sad this would have made William to know he had done so much for so many, but yet no one cared enough to see him off and to say farewell. The service was very short and when the minister had finished he turned to Susan and told her they would give her a moment alone with him before placing him in the ground. After they had walked away she walked toward the casket that was waiting to be lowered into the ground and placed her hand there to say goodbye. It was then something amazing happened.

William spoke to her in her mind and said, "I wish to thank you for coming to see me off and for bringing me the stone. I am with my family now and I will be eternally grateful to you for the peace you have brought to me."

Now, tears flowing hard once again, hardly able to see when she opened her eyes, she opened her hand and the stone was there once again. She did not understand how this was possible, but after all she had seen and done, it was clear to her anything was possible through faith. As she closed her eyes once again and squeezed the stone tightly, she prayed one last time and said goodbye to William and wished him well. When her eyes opened she was back at the old school house sitting in one of the desks. As she turned to the right she noticed someone there with his head down on one of the desks sleeping as if he were waiting for her to return. It was none other than Norman, who had made his way to the old schoolhouse during the storm in search of her.

She reached out and touched him on the shoulder and he raised his head, cleared his eyes and said, "Good to have you back Susan. I was wondering how long you were going to be gone."

She asked, "How long have I been gone?"

Norman replied, "Only through the night, as the hurricane reached its full punch, but it seems the worst is over now. I think we can make our way back to the old house if it is still standing."

They both rose to their feet and opened the door to see the house was still standing and noticed Sara and Robert making their way toward the old schoolhouse, to check on them as well. It was then Susan opened her hand and realized she was still holding onto the rock with William and Annie's names engraved. And in her pocket she found the one remaining silver dollar that she would cherish forever.

After they returned to the house Susan told everyone there all about her adventure and about the life of William and his family and his gift. Little did she know that very day standing there at his grave, he had indeed passed her his gift as well, now it would only be a matter of time until she would discover what he had done.

The Picture

It was five fifteen in the morning and soon the sun would be shining in from the east windows of the old estate. Norman's sister Sherry had been up all night long because something had made her a bit restless during the night, but she wasn't able to completely understand what it was. The wind had been howling all night long, as the cold air of winter had closed in on the old estate. Norman and all the others had gone away for a week or so and she stayed behind because of a few other commitments and because she simply wanted some time to herself to think a few things through. She was not completely alone in the house however, the two dogs were there to keep her company along with dear old Rex.

Something about that darn bird just gave everyone the willies, maybe it was that same old black stare that he had in his eyes no matter what it was that he was thinking. It was never hard to tell when he was up to something, he would always cock his head from side to side as if he was reading your mind. Sherry looked over at him as he sat there staring back at her doing just that, leaning his head from one side then to the other as she looked at him. It was almost as if he could tell something was bothering her.

She had just come in from the barn about an hour ago where she had been playing her heart out as she gently caressed the ivory keys of the piano. She felt so at peace as the music flowed from her very heart and soul and to her fingertips and out into the air. When she opened her eyes she couldn't help but notice all the little critters of the outdoors that had gathered around to listen as she played. She had heard her brother Norman speak of them before, but no one else had really seen them. There was a raccoon that sat there at the small opening of the doorway with his hands crossed as if he was praying, and a rabbit standing at his side. Then up in the rafters she could see the old owl that seemed to sway with the music almost as if he could feel it running through his veins. As she walked out the door to head back up to the old estate, she noticed just outside the door stood a mother deer with her fawn who had been listening as well. It seemed they were not frightened at all and never made an attempt to scamper off even as she walked out the door and toward the house. She looked back several times on her way back to the house and noticed they all just stood there together watching as if to make sure she made it back safely.

Once back inside she headed up to the den and sat down at the computer and started reading a short story that had been written and sent to her from a friend she had recently met. There was something about the words within his stories that captivated her, almost as if they were speaking directly to her. Most had found this to be true that had read along through the years, each having a message or lesson hidden between the lines. Little did any of them know that these stories carried more fact than fiction; sure there was plenty of fiction, but hidden there between those lines the truth could be found about each and every one who played a part within the story.

Just as the sun began to peer through the east windows of the estate, Rex began to caw as if something was bothering him. Sherry walked over to his cage but was a little afraid to touch it, so she spoke softly to him hoping it would calm him, and it seemed to work very well. She then returned to the story that she was about to finish. After finishing she sat there for a moment to gather her thoughts and tried to put all the pieces together from the story to try to understand this writer just a bit more. It was not that she did not understand what his stories were about, but she wanted to know more about him as a man and what drove him to write about the things that he had for so very long now.

As she turned to look back at Rex she couldn't believe her eyes, he had vanished out of thin air. The cage door was still closed and locked but Rex was nowhere to be found. For the first time all night she spoke out, "Oh great, now that crazy bird is on the loose somewhere in the house. That's all I need."

Slowly, one room at a time she searched for old Rex, but not a sign of him could be found. She knew the house was big enough that she might have just missed him or he might have been able to avoid her if that was what he was trying to do. Then as she came round the corner, there it was, the door in the corridor was opened. It was the door leading downstairs into the cobblestone room. She had heard about it from all of the tales from the others, but had never ventured down there herself, nor did she really care to at this point. But she could hear the sound of Rex cawing down below as if he was calling out her name. At first she was a little afraid to venture down, but then she thought back of all the stories the others had told and none of them had even been harmed in any way, so why should she fear anything at all.

Step by step she slowly made her way down the stairs and as she reached the floor below, she looked closely for any sign of Rex. She thought to herself, how in the world would someone call a raven anyway, as she made a silly attempt to make a cawing sound like Rex. It was then she heard him sending back a caw of his own. Very hesitant about stepping on the stones of the floor she gently placed her foot on the stone before her and then another and then another surprised that nothing had happened up to this point. It was then she heard a noise coming from upstairs. As she stopped dead in her tracks and listened closely, she hoped it was someone who had returned and could help her.

Upstairs Robert had returned home early and had entered the house hoping to find Sherry sitting comfortably in the den. It was no surprise to him to see that she was not there, at first he thought to himself that maybe she had gone down to the harbor. But it was then that he noticed old Rex was not in his cage, and his heart began to race just thinking about what he might have gotten Sherry into while they were all away. He shouted out loud, "You damn crazy bird, what have you done now?"

He knew just where to look first and headed for the doorway of the corridor down below. As he came around the corner he could see that the door was opened and he stuck his head inside and yelled, "Sherry, are you down there?"

Sherry stood perfectly still and answered, "Yes, Robert, I am down here and I think Rex is down here too."

Robert shot through the doorway and down the steps just short of the floor, careful to not touch the stones below. He was very surprised to see that Sherry had already stepped out into the cobblestone floor and nothing had happened. She was just out of his reach, yet he reached for her as he said, "Sherry do not take another step, you never know what stone it will be that will send you off into the unknown."

Sherry just smiled and answered, "It is alright Robert, I am not afraid."

As they stood there looking at each other trying to think of what to do Rex came walking out of the dark from the adjoining cobblestone room. He stopped for a moment and looked at Robert and cocked his head to the side, and made a noise that sounded as if he was laughing. This sound sent chills down Robert's spine as he shouted, "Don't you dare, you crazy bird or I will fry you like a chicken."

Rex stood there for a second and then hopped over to the feet of Sherry and then looked back at Robert one last time. He then turned his head and pecked at the stone that Sherry's left foot was standing on. All of the floor except for stones they were standing on seemed to begin to move and flow like water as Robert and Sherry made eye contact one last time. As she started to drift farther away Robert made a final attempt to reach her before it was too late. But as he dove for her he landed in the floor which had turned to a muddy mortar mix, slipping and sliding as he tried to get up to his feet. When he climbed back onto the solid stairs he turned back and Sherry and Rex had vanished out of sight.

Robert was covered in the muddy mortar mess and as he made his way back up the stairs he mumbled, "Boy, oh boy, Norman's going to be mad at me when he hears about this."

By the time he reached the top of the stairs Norman, Sara and Susan were coming down the hallway asking what the Sam Hell was going on. Robert did his best to explain, but all he could say was that Rex had taken Sherry away. They all walked down the cobblestone steps together as they stood in silence wondering just where Rex had taken her off to and how long it would be before she would return.

In what seemed to be a flash and less than a second, Sherry found herself standing outside where the sun was shining brightly. The air was warm as the breeze blew across her face and rustled through her long silky hair. She looked around for Rex, but he was nowhere to be found; obviously he did not make the trip with her and she was here all alone. She then looked down to her watch to notice that the time had changed as well. It was now seven fifty in the morning, and as she looked around she couldn't help but notice that it seemed that she was on some kind of military base. She could see planes all lined up in perfect rows like they were waiting for someone to jump into them and take off.

It was then she heard a roar in the distance. The sound began to fill the air, and what started off as a buzz was quickly turning into a roar. Then she could hear what sounded like great explosions that seemed to shake the ground and then all hell broke loose. The planes came crashing in from the harbor where most of the Pacific fleet had been docked. It was then that one hundred and eighty three Japanese planes rumbled across the Southern coast of the island of Oahu. She recognized this from history and knew she had landed smack dab in the middle of the attack on Pearl Harbor. It was now five minutes to eight, December the seventh, nineteen forty one and everyone was running everywhere as no one had seen this coming. She spoke softly to herself, "If only I could have been here sooner I could have warned the others. But I know that was not the purpose for Rex sending me here. What could it be?"

The roar in the air at this point was so loud all she could do was duck and cover her ears and hope she was not in any danger. She had managed to run over to a jeep and kneel down beside it to take cover from the hail of bullets flying everywhere. She raised her head and looked around whenever she had the chance, but some of the planes on the ground had been hit and hit hard. They exploded into flames, causing her to keep her head down most of the time. She could see as the pilots ran for their planes to try to get them into the air and off the ground to have a fighting chance. Many of them were cut down before they even reached their planes and others never got them off the ground at all. If the Japanese pilots ran out of ammunition they simply crashed their planes into what ever they could find to cause the most damage or destruction. It was clear to see that the Americans had been caught completely off guard and so had Sherry as to why she was here seeing this.

In what seemed to last forever, the attack pounded on with such great force that she could feel the percussion in her chest as each explosion took place. At times she found herself blinded by the dust and smoke from all that was happening.

In less than two hours the attack came to an end although it seemed to last forever. The smoke from the coastline blackened the sky from the ships that were still on fire, and explosions could still be heard as they burned in the harbor. When all was done, two thousand two hundred and eighty service men were dead and sixty-eight civilians as well.

Sherry couldn't believe the devastation that she has just witnessed as she walked about the base looking to see if there was anyone she could help. It was then a few hundred feet from where she had been kneeling beside the jeep she found Airman Mike Holmes as he laid there on the ground. He had been shot and was bleeding very badly so she knelt down beside him. He reached out to her and grasped her hand. It was clear to see that Mike was not going to make it and it was amazing that he had even held on for this long with the injuries that he had suffered.

The sun was behind Sherry when she knelt down beside Mike and he grasped her hand. All he could see was a silhouette of her as the sun radiated from behind, and he asked, "Are you an angel?"

Sherry, with tears in her eyes, not wanting to crush his hopes answered, "Yes, I guess I am today. Please hang on and I will try to get someone to help you."

Mike just stared at her as the light radiated from behind her silhouette and said, "No, it is too late for that now, I know I will be leaving here shortly. Do not worry, I am not in pain any longer, all I need is for you to do something for me."

Sherry wiped the tears from her eyes and replied, "Yes, anything my dear man, anything at all."

Mike then reached up and unbuttoned his shirt pocket and pulled a letter from it and handed to her and asked, "Would you please get this letter and picture inside to my darling wife and tell her that I am sorry, and that I will love her forever."

Sherry took the letter from his hand and smiled as the tears flowed down her face and said, "Yes, I will make sure your letter is delivered, I will deliver it myself."

Mike smiled and said, "Thank you my angel, now I think it's time to take me home."

It was then Mike's hand went limp and lost its grip with Sherry's. He had lost his battle with life and had set himself free of this world and all that held him here. Sherry sat with him for a while longer until someone came to take him away. Now she knew why old Rex had sent her here on this moment of history; It was to be there for Mike so he did not die alone and so that his final letter and picture would make its way back home. As she stood there staring down at the letter she couldn't help wonder how this could all be possible. How was she to deliver a letter to someone when she returned that may not even be alive themselves so many years later. Then while staring at the letter there was a bright flash of light so bright and blue it was blinding to the eyes and she was gone, just as quickly as she had come.

The next thing Sherry knew she felt something pecking her gently almost as if to waken her from a deep sleep. When she opened her eyes there was old Rex standing beside her as she sat there on the cobblestone floor of the old estate. She heard a rumbling of movement as Norman, Sara, Robert and Susan came charging down the stairs careful not to touch the floor at the bottom. They stopped short and stood and stared at Sherry as she sat there on the floor, all so happy to see that she had returned safely. Sherry still with tears in her eyes, smiled at them. She then looked back down to her hand to notice the letter gripped tightly between her fingers and the palm of her hand. She then clutched it close to her heart almost as if she was afraid someone was going to take it from her or it would vanish if she let it go.

She climbed to her feet and started walking toward the steps where all the others were waiting patiently to hear about the journey she had taken. It was then that Rex shot past her and all the others and up the stairs with Robert close behind yelling something about fried chicken again. All the others couldn't help but laugh, even Sherry as she climbed her way back up the stairs and to the kitchen where they would all sit and listen to what she had experienced while way.

As she sat there and told them all that had happened, she clutched the letter even tighter in her hand. When finished telling all about the journey, she opened her hand and rolled the letter over and noticed the name and address on the front. The only thing that was missing was the stamp he needed for him to have mailed it that morning of the attack. She figured that was why it was still in his pocket and not on its way to his dear wife. As she stood there looking at the address she said, "Looks like I will be heading for Chicago first thing in the morning."

Norman never questioned her motives at all after hearing her story, he simply replied, "I will call and make the arrangements. I will be going with you this time."

Sherry thanked him and the others for being there for her, and then excused herself to go get some rest before they had to leave in the morning.

Bright and early the next morning Norman and Sherry boarded the flight to Chicago. If they were lucky, in just a couple of hours they would have more answers to the pieces of this magnificent puzzle. During the flight Sherry sat there and told Norman one more time all that had happened as he sat there listening and felt her every word. He found himself just as curious as they both wondered what this letter could be all about and what purpose could it possibly serve after all of these years.

When they landed they had a car there waiting to pick them up, Norman had made sure all the arrangements had been made so this trip could go without a hitch. They then directed the driver who was familiar with the area to the address in the old part of the city. When they arrived at the address, Norman stepped from the car and helped Sherry out as well. At this point Sherry had taken out the letter and was once again holding it tightly in her hand and felt as if she had just left Mike's side only moments ago, even though he had passed away sixty four years ago.

Sherry gently knocked on the door and woman who looked to be in her late fifties opened the door and said, "Yes, can I help you?"

Sherry looked her right in the eyes and said, "Hello, my name is Sherry and this is my brother Norman. I was hoping you could help me locate Mrs. Holmes?"

The woman hesitated for a moment and then answered, "I am sorry, but Mrs. Holmes passed away about thirty years ago."

As tears welled up in her eyes and fist clinched tighter against the letter she asked, "Can you tell me anything about her, anything at all?"

The woman stuck out her hand and said, "I am sorry, my name is Ruth Ann. I have lived here all of my life and my parents have always lived next door. Mrs. Holmes was always a very kind and gentle woman and always kept to herself."

Sherry asked, "By any chance do you know if she was ever married?"

Ruth Ann smiled and said, "Yes, my mother told me that she was married but her husband was killed during the war and she never remarried after that."

Sherry then asked, "Did you buy this house from her?"

Ruth Ann answered, "No, I bought it from her son after she passed away."

A bit confused Sherry asked, "Her son, I though you said she never remarried."

Ruth Ann smile and replied, "That's what I said, what I didn't say was that she was two months pregnant when her husband left for Oahu, where he had been stationed. She only had the chance to notify him that she was with child the day before he died."

With her heart beating all the way up into her throat Sherry asked, "Do you know where I could find her son?"

Once again Ruth Ann, with a smirk of a smile on her face answered, "Mike, yes I know where he is, at least that's where he was when I bought the house from him. But I do not know if he is still alive. He would be around sixty four or five years old by now."

Sherry thought about that for a second and then asked, "Would you please tell me where that might be."

Ruth Ann answered, "He lives in Hawaii, the island of Oahu where his father died. He had no other living relatives and had never met his father so he moved there to be close to where he had died, just to be feel closer to him."

Sherry thanked her for all she had shared with them and turned and headed back for the car that was waiting in front of the house for them. Sherry and Norman knew they had no choice now but to head out on the first plane for Oahu and hope that Mike was not only still there but still alive as well. She would not rest until she had made every attempt to deliver this letter and picture to Mike's only living relative, his son.

From Chicago it was a grueling eight hour non-stop flight to Oahu, but at least they could get some sleep while the flight was in the air. That was something they were both going to need by the time the flight landed in Hawaii. This also gave the both of them time to absorb the information that Ruth Ann had shared with them, after all when they started this journey they had no idea at all that there was a son involved.

After a long night of sleeping peacefully during their flight they had reached their destination and the sun was shining brightly as it always did after the brief early morning shower that seemed to always kiss the island. In a matter of moments that moisture was gone and the rest of the day was always dry and warm.

Just after landing, the two of them walked straight over to the closest phone and Sherry picked up the phone book. Norman reached for it but hesitated as he started thinking about how many other people had probably had their hands all over the darn thing. Sherry wasn't too happy about touching it either, but she was driven by her curiosity to see if he was listed or still lived there at all. As she turned the pages there it was, Michael Holmes, Jr. almost as if it jumped out at her. Her heart began to pound as she turned to Norman and told him the news. She pulled a pen and paper from her purse and jotted down the address and then the two of them marched their way to the counter to find a car to rent for the day.

As they drove about the island they had to stop several times to get directions as to how get to where Mike lived. Ironically it was not far at all from the same base where his father had been killed during the attack so many years ago. It was in a very nice area on the island and it looked as if most of the homes there had been built within the past few years. So it was hard telling where he had been living on the island before that.

They stepped from the car and slowly walked up to the door where Mike was now living, not at all knowing what to expect or how he would receive them or talk to them at all. Sherry had no idea at all how she was going to explain how she came across this letter after all of these years. She wasn't sure there was a chance in hell in him believing how Rex took her on a journey back in time just to get this letter and then brought her back home. They both stood there at the door looking at each other as if they were both having the same thought. Then Norman reached up and pressed the button to the door bell and they heard it ring inside the house. After a few seconds the door opened and a man who seemed to be in his mid sixties stood before them.

The man said, "Hello, can I help you?"

Sherry smiled and replied, "It is you that I hope I can help, is your name Mike Holmes, Jr. by any chance?"

Mike smiled and answered, "Why yes, it is and I am always willing to take all the help I can get," as he chuckled.

They all stood there and shook each others hands and introduced themselves and then asked if they could come in and tell him their story. At first Mike wasn't too sure he wanted to let them in and hear any story at all, until Sherry mentioned it was about his father. When he heard those words he opened the door wide and asked them to please come in and share with him their story.

He offered them a seat and before sitting himself he asked them if they would like something to drink before starting. They thanked him for asking but said that would not be necessary.

Mike then sat down across from them in what seemed to be his favorite chair. He then asked, "Now what's this all about, that you have a story to tell about my father?"

Sherry pulled the letter from her purse and held it in her hand once again. She looked at Mike and said, "I have a story to tell you before I hand you this letter, one you may or may not believe, but it is very true."

With a puzzled look upon his face Mike replied, "Please go on, I am always willing to hear anything about my father anytime anyone is willing to tell me. After all everyone who knew my father has passed away and I am the only twig left on this family tree."

Sherry then proceeded in telling him all about how strangely enough she had been thrown back in time and found herself there the day the attack took place. She did not expose that it was the cobblestone room that took her there. She simply told him how in a flash she found herself there moments before the attack took place and did not know why, at least not until she was handed the letter. She told him all about what she had seen and how much it meant to his father for this letter to be delivered. With tears flowing from her eyes she then told him about how his father and all the others had died that day with honor doing their best to get to the planes. She then handed Mike the letter and told him that it was handed to her by his father as he asked her to make sure to give it to his wife and tell her that he loved her.

As Mike took the letter you could see that he was a bit confused. No matter how much he wanted to believe that someone like Sherry was there comforting his father when he left this world, it was all a little hard to believe it could be possible. But as he looked down at the letter he couldn't help noticing how old and frail it seemed to be. It was clear that this letter that he held in his hands had been written long ago. The address on the front was addressed to his mother and there was something about holding it in is hand that made him feel good, but he didn't know why. Maybe just thinking that it had at one time been in his father's hand as well was enough to comfort him.

As Sherry and Norman sat there, they watched Mike reach over and pick up his letter opener and carefully open the letter from the end. He was very careful to not cause any more damage to the envelope than necessary to get the contents out. As he carefully pulled the letter from the envelope a picture fell into his lap. He reached down and picked it up and couldn't believe his eyes, at that age he had looked just like his father. Mike did his best to hold back his emotions but they could see that it was everything that he could do. It was as he read the letter aloud that he could not hold them back anymore, as the tears poured from his eyes and his tears feel upon the single page letter that he was reading.

My Dear Barbra,

> I know it has only been a few months since we have been together, but I have missed you so. The weather here is warm and sunny most of the time, but it is the warmth and ray of sunshine that you bring to my life that I miss the most. I am sorry I am unable to be there with you as you go through these months carrying our child. Please whisper to him softly each night that I love him. Yes, I know we do not know what the baby will be yet, but for some reason I have a feeling that it is going to be a boy. I don't know why but when I closed my eyes

and fell to sleep last night I saw you standing with the light behind you and you were holding a small young boy. I know it was just a dream, but seemed so very real to me when I woke in this morning. I know that you do not have a picture of me, so I am sending you this one that I just received yesterday. If for some reason I am not there, please show Mike Jr. my picture everyday and tell him that his father loves him more than life itself and that I would be there if there was any way possible. That is, if you are alright with calling him Mike. There seems to be a lot of commotion going on outside so I will end this letter now, but remember I will love you always my dear, and with hopes to see you soon.

Love, Mike

Mike folded the letter gently and placed it back into the envelope as he looked back at Norman and Sherry and noticed they both were unable to hold back their tears as well. Mike then said, "I do not know how this was possible, but you have brought to me the most precious gift that I could ever receive. I also want you to know I believe every word you have shared with me today and I thank you for what you have done. You have brought peace to an old man, who has been searching for this peace all of his life. "

With tears still steaming down her lovely face Sherry answered, "It was a pleasure for me to spend those final moments with your father and for also spending this time with you."

Mike then asked, "Would you do me one last favor if you have the time?"

Without hesitation Sherry answered, "Yes, Mike, I would be happy to help anyway I can."

As he placed the picture gently on the shelf along side of the picture of his mother he turned and asked, "Would it be at all possible for you to take me to where it was that my father died that day so long ago?"

A little confused Sherry replied, "Mike, I am not sure they will even let us on the base, let alone would I be able to remember the spot."

Mike answered, "Don't worry about the base, I have friends that can get us on if you are willing to try to find the spot."

Sherry agreed and instantly Mike picked up the phone and called someone he knew from the base and they told him that they would meet them at the gate and take them wherever they needed to go.

When they arrived at the gate Mike's friend was there waiting and Sherry then asked the gentleman to take them to where the planes would have been parked along the runway during the time of the attack. When they arrived much to Sherry's surprise it all came back to her because most of the buildings had remained and had been kept the same, bullet holes and all. It was almost as if something or someone was pulling her and directing her to the spot she was searching for. Then she not only found it, but could feel it as well, as she pointed to the area where Mike had laid that morning and spoke his final words. Mike Jr. walked over to the spot and knelt down and placed both hands on the ground as he poured his heart and soul out and could not hold back the tears once again. He then kissed the ground and thanked his father for the picture and said out loud for all to hear, "I love you, Dad!"

It was clear as they all walked away that Mike had finally made peace with the things in life he searched for. It was also very clear to Sherry because now she knew and understood the purpose for her journey from the cobblestone room. It was not that she would ever want to step on another stone or feel more comfortable being around Rex, but happy just the same that she had made the journey.

Norman and Sherry returned home and found the others all waiting when they arrived. They all sat as they always did after returning and shared what they had learned with each other, leaving questions in all of their minds as to who would be chosen next and where that journey may lead. They all sat there listening to Rex who was in the other room and out of view, cawing almost as if he were laughing, sending cold chills down their spines.

Into the Fog

Once again late fall had settled in on Northern Wisconsin and the air was cool and damp as Red and Jim slid across the water in their boat. They were slowly heading out of the cove where their cabin could be found. They looked through the opening between the trees to the main body of water and saw that the fog had settled in as thick as it was the first time they had been lost. They knew once they crossed past the little boat house on the point there would be no coming back until they had finished their journey. They sat there in the light fog of the cove and decided to talk a little before crossing over to the point of no return. They knew the fog had come for them for a reason, but they were a little curious as to what that reason might be this time.

After sitting there and talking for a few more minutes, Red asked, "Well what do you think, should we go for it and see what it has in store for us this time."

Jim smiled and answered, "Sure why not, besides I have a feeling that if we don't go to it, then it will come for us anyway."

Red shifted the motor into gear and slowly powered his way out of the cove and past the small white boat house and out in the deep thick fog. Just as before it was so thick they could not see each other in the boat. Heck, they couldn't even see their own hand when they held it up and tried. Once again they could hear each other but could not see a thing. As they sat there talking Jim noticed that it seemed if the longer they talked the farther Red's voice seemed to be drifting away, almost as if they had been separated. He couldn't understand how this was at all possible, after all they were in the same boat and had entered the fog together.

In a matter of only a few moments Jim realized Red was no longer drifting along with him, he was now alone. The sounds that drift for miles across the water could no longer be heard and the fog felt as if it was lifting him up and carrying him off. It was then that he realized it wasn't Red who was drifting away it was himself, as his heart began to race. Then a feeling of calm came over him like he had never felt before and he felt something at his feet almost as if he had been placed gently upon solid ground, but he still could not see a thing. He stood there motionless afraid to move, wondering what might be there once the fog had lifted. As he stood there blinded by the fog he couldn't help but wonder if Red was still sitting in the boat or had been whisked off somewhere on his own. One thing that was perfectly clear was that they were no longer together anymore.

Slowly Jim noticed the fog started to lift and he started to be able to see the outline of what was before his eyes. He stood on what appeared to be a dirt road with two strips that seemed as if they were from wagon wheels. It was obvious that they were not tire tracks because they were too narrow for that, it was the only thing they could have been. It was clear the road had been used very much because the grass along the edges was rather high, but on the road it was very short. He also noticed that the weeds were very high along the edge of what appeared to be fields that lined both sides of the road. As a matter of fact, he could not see over the mixture of growth to even see where he might be, so he started walking, hoping to find something up around what appeared to be a bend in the road.

Meanwhile as Red sat there in the boat he also couldn't help but notice that he could no longer hear Jim's voice in the boat. He also had felt a shift of weight as if the front end of the boat where Jim had been sitting had come up and was lighter in the water. He knew he had not fallen into the water because he never heard a thing, he would have clearly heard the splash if that would have happened. As the fog began to lift around him he noticed once again just as before, the cabins were all gone, even the little white boat house that sat at the opening of the cove that lead back to their old cabin. It was then he noticed Jim was indeed no longer in the boat and he was alone as well. He couldn't help but wonder where Jim had been taken and he also couldn't help but wonder at what point and time he had been sent to as well.

Not knowing what to do, Red dropped a line in the water and thought that he would go ahead and fish for awhile and wait to see what this time and place had in store for him. He knew he was a very patient man and he could sit out there and fish as long as it would take and be perfectly happy doing so. After a few moments had passed he noticed that he had a bite on the line that he had dropped in the water. At first it didn't appear to be much of a bite or enough to get him excited, but the fact that you never know what it might be was enough to draw his interest. He waited patiently for it to nibble once again and it was then the line shot across the water and the rod bent in his hands as he held on tightly. Never before had he felt such power and force as it pulled against him and his hands struggled to hold on. His line was strong and he did not have any fears of it giving way or breaking and losing what he had managed to hook, but it was pulling with such force that it started moving the boat slowly about the lake. Now his heart was pounding in his chest and he tried to imagine in his own mind what could possibly have this much strength and power. All of his life he dreamed of hooking something like this and now it had happened. He fought and held on as the boat continued to be pulled around the lake, all day and into the night as his hands grew weary but he would not let go. As he mumbled aloud, "You might as well wear yourself out my friend because I am never going to give up on you, you will be the one to give up before I do."

It was then, that what ever it was that had been pulling him stopped and held the line tight. Red tried to pull it to the surface but it pulled back with the same force, simply holding him at bay as his hands began to tremble with exhaustion. With it simply holding the line tightly he found he was able to release the pole with one hand and hold it with the other and have a chance at least to rest one arm and hand at a time. It was almost as if whatever it was had decided to let him rest before continuing on with the fight.

Now Jim had managed to make his way around the bend in the road and could see what appeared to be a large white house up the road a ways. It had big white pillars similar to the old plantation homes many, many years ago. As he walked closer he could hear what sounded like someone whistling a tune, but one that sounded like no other he had heard before, but yet one that seemed to soothe his very soul. He found himself being drawn in by the tune as he continued to walk down the dirt road and closer to the big white house. It was then he could barely make out what appeared to be two young men sitting at a table on the front porch. With each step things became clearer as to what the two young men were doing. One was leaning back in his old wooden chair whistling the tune that had drawn him around the bend and toward the house. The other was waving at him motioning for him to come join them at the table. Yes, now he could see there was a third chair at the table on the porch, almost as if they knew he was coming.

As he walked up to the house, the eldest of the two young men stood and walked toward him and stuck out his hand and said, "Welcome my brother, we have been waiting patiently for you to arrive."

Jim shook his hand and said, "Hello my name is Jim, could you kindly tell me where I am?"

He replied, "My name is Elijua, and this is Joshua, we are your brothers and we are here to help you find what it is you are looking for."

Joshua jumped to his feet as well and shook Jim's hand and it was very easy for him to tell he was happy to see him as well."

Jim then asked, "What do you mean you are my brothers?"

Elijua laughed and said, "We have always been brothers of the spirit and at one time we were all together many, many years ago. But as the years have passed, we have all been sent back at different places and times to do the work we were meant to do."

It was clear to see by both Elijua and Joshua that Jim was very confused, so they invited him to sit down and share a drink of wine with them before they continue on. The wine was in what appeared to be a very old handmade pottery flask and there were three pottery mugs on the table

152 / James H. Pierce

as well. Joshua poured the wine into all three mugs and slid one over to each of them.

It was then, as Jim sat there completely puzzled as to what was going on and where he was at, politely said, "I am sorry I do not drink and have not for many years now."

Elijua smiled and said, "Drink my brother, that does not matter here, the Lord has always told us to drink a little for thy stomach sake."

A little hesitant Jim reached out and clanged his mug together with the other two in the air, waiting as Joshua said, "To the return of our brother Jim, and to his safe journey home."

Jim lifted his mug to his mouth as they did the same and for the first time in twenty five years he tasted the wine as it touched his lips and then his tongue bringing back so many memories of things he had long forgotten. There was something magical about the wine as his memories of lives past flowed freely through his mind and he remembered clearly the time the three of them had spent together so very long ago.

Elijua and Joshua just sat back and smiled watching Jim's eyes come alive as he recognized and remembered them both. As they sat there and finished their flask of wine they talked about all of their journeys through the past and all of the lives they have touched and the work that they had done through time. Jim never felt more at home than he did at this moment and he was very grateful for having the chance to see his brothers of the spirit once again.

After finishing the wine and talking for what seemed to be hours, Jim asked, "So what am I here for, do you know?"

Joshua spoke up quickly and said, "It is just as Elijua had told you earlier. We are here to help you find what you are looking for."

Jim, still a little confused by his answer replied, "Ok, Ok I get that part, but how do we find something when I don't even know what it is we are looking for?"

With a smile on his face Elijua answered, "Do not worry yourself about this my brother, you will know when you find it."

Jim just sat back in his chair and finished off his wine; At this point none of this was making any sense. So rather than continue to ask questions without answers he figured he would just wait and see what they had in store for him next.

Now in the dark of night, Red found himself still holding the fishing rod with line still tight. He had managed to tuck it under his arm to give his hands a rest. It would tug a little every now and then but held a constant strain on the line at all times, whatever it could be. The clouds had blackened the sky and did not allow even the light of a single star to shine through, leaving Red sitting in an unknown time and place on the lake, feeling no better than he had sitting it the blinding fog. At least there he could see the fog, here it felt as if the darkness had closed in on him and was almost reaching out to touch him. The only thing that kept him awake was the movement on the line every time he started to lose his concentration. It was almost as if whatever it could be was toying with him, just to see how far he was willing to go before giving in. But in the back of his mind he knew that would never happen, sooner or later he knew, it was going to get the best of him or he was going to get the best of it.

As night began to turn to day the sun peeked over the horizon and through the thick trees along the shoreline. Red reached down with one hand and cupped a handful of water and rubbed it across his face, then another, then another until he felt awake and ready for more. Just then the line pulled harder and the pole bent even more, dragging the boat across the sun-lit waters once again. Red couldn't believe what he was seeing or feeling but he would not have missed this for the world. Both hands now held on to the rod and reel gripped between his thighs to help him hang on. Every now and then it would pause just long enough to give him the rest that he needed and then off they would go again. He had grown hungry and thirsty, but it was not enough to make him give up on his fight today or ever. He even found himself talking to the fish saying, "Come on big boy, come to old Red. I will not hurt you, I promise to set you free when we are done."

Jim, Elijua and Joshua, in the light of the oil lamp sat on the porch through the night talking and laughing about time gone by as they did their best to help Jim remember all that he had forgotten. Then as the sunlight lit up the day Joshua picked up the lamp and motioned for Jim to follow, and he did while Elijua followed close behind. They entered the house and walked directly to what appeared to be a doorway opened to the steps that led beneath the house. As they walked down the stairs Jim couldn't help but notice that there were several levels to the basement. Each time he stopped, Joshua motioned for him to continue to follow so he and Elijua would not be left back in the dark. There were no windows obviously because of the depth they had traveled so the lamp was the only light that could be seen anymore.

Then at what appeared to be the third level below, Joshua reached for the door and turned the knob and threw his shoulder into it to force it open. It was clear to see that it had been many, many years since anyone had entered that room. Jim and Elijua followed Joshua into the room and as held the lamp high into the air, Jim couldn't believe his eyes. The room was stacked with layers and layers of wooden crates. The only clearing was a path down the middle of the room.

Jim started to laugh and said, "You have got to be kidding me, how in the hell are we going to know which crate we are suppose to open to find what I am here to find?"

With that Joshua and Elijua couldn't help but laugh and then they all found themselves laughing together as Jim joined in. Then after they all settled down a bit, they began opening the crates one at a time hoping that whatever it was that Jim was there to find would become obvious when it was found. After searching through crates and boxes through most of the day, they realized they had hardly made a dent in what was all there. It was then Joshua dimmed the light of the lamp and it was clear to see at the far end of the path beneath several other crates, a light could be seen. Jim was amazed that something that had been closed up down here for that long could be glowing at all. It clearly couldn't be a lamp, nothing could have held that much oil. In the darkness they all walked toward the glowing crate and when they reached it Joshua turned the light of the lamp back up so they could see clearly to move the others crates that sat up on top.

As Joshua and Elijua stood to the side, Jim began to open the glowing crate, unsure of what he might find as he pulled the boards free. Then as the lid came pulling loose it was clear it was filled with several pieces of clothing. Inside he found a very old hat, overcoat, pants and shoes that looked as if it had come from his time, not these years of the past. He couldn't help but wonder how this was at all possible. As he continued to pull the clothes out of the crate he noticed what appeared to be a big red suit lined in white with a white wig and a beard to match, all the way down to the red hat and black boots and bells that hung from the sides of the coat. He didn't have to wonder what this was, he knew very well this was a Santa suit, but yet it looked almost brand new if he didn't know better. Then as he lifted the clothes one at a time to place them back into the crate, a letter fell from the old overcoat. It read, "Take these garments and use them wisely, one will allow you to go places others would not want to go and places others will ask you to leave, so you can help the weak and wearies of my flock. The other will allow you to go places others cannot and open doors that would normally be closed. Use this garment to touch the lives of the innocent and by doing so you will fill them with hopes and dreams and take away their pain and sorrow. Let no one know who you are as you go about your way and I will give you all that you need to continue on with your work."

Joshua and Elijua just stood there with a smile on their faces and watched as Jim sat down and wrapped his arms around the crate that he now held on his lap. It was then the lamp went dark and Jim could not see a thing. He yelled out several times for Joshua and Elijua but they did not answer back, he heard nothing and the dark was pitch black, not even the crate that he held in his arms was glowing any longer. He sat there in the dark patiently waiting, just as Red had the night before in the dark of night, feeling as if the darkness could reach out and touch him.

Red had managed to fight the fish through another day as he watched his hands begin to bleed and the skin tear from his palms. He would not give in, not after all he had endure and the fight they had shared. Then the line went limp, almost as if it had been cut or broken. But that wasn't what was happening at all. Whatever it was he noticed was coming up straight at him, heading for the boat at an unbelievable speed. He couldn't even reel the line in fast enough to keep up. Then out of the water shot what appeared to be an angel with wings so white they were blinding as the light of day faded behind the trees and nightfall closed in. It floated down and sat in the front of the boat where Jim had been sitting before he had vanished.

The angel sat there and looked into Red's eyes and said, "You have been a great fisherman and have fought with all of your heart and soul, yet I have only held your line between my thumb and finger gently."

Red looked down at the angels hand and noticed what she was saying was true. She simply had the line pinched between her finger and thumb. He then looked down to his own hands and noticed the blood and skin that had been torn from them and said, "Thank you for the fight, but why have you brought me here and challenged me so?"

The angel smiled and answered, "Because you are a fisherman and it is what all fishermen live for, the fight and the challenges that lay ahead. You are also a fisherman of men and if you fight as hard for the souls of all of those paths you cross, you will clearly have given our Lord your best and you shall be rewarded with his kingdom."

Now the night had closed in on Red once again and the only light that could be found was from the glow of the angel's wings. Red nodded his head and smiled showing the angel he clearly understood what it was he was sent here to learn.

The angel then reached out and touched both of his hands and they were instantly healed, the cuts and blood were gone as if it never happened at all. Then in the twinkling of an eye the light of the angel's wings was gone and the black of night was upon him once again; He couldn't even see his hand in front of his face. Red found himself very tired and curled up in the bottom of the boat and slipped off to sleep, waking just before sunup and watched for the light to peek through the trees. As the light started to clear his vision he looked and noticed Jim sitting back in his seat sleeping holding what appeared to be a wooded crate in his lap. Red just sat there and watched him until he opened his eyes and noticed he was back in the boat. It was clear to see in both of their eyes that they were happy to see each other once again. As they looked around it was then that Red noticed he could see the little white boat house that led into the cove and back to their cabin.

Red looked at Jim and said, "Welcome home my friend."

Jim smiled still clutching onto his crate and said, "Yes, welcome home to you as well my old friend."

Quietly and slowly, in the peacefulness of the morning light, they made their way back into the cove and back to the cabin. There they sat for hours and told each other about where they had been and what they had seen. Jim showed Red the note that was inside the crate and the clothes he had been given. Red smiled as if he clearly understood why Jim had gone on his journey into the fog. As Red told his story about the struggle and how the angel had come to him and what she had said, Jim smiled as well knowing that they had both been touched by the spirit while on their journeys in the fog.

Still to this day Red continues to reach out to those souls that have lost their way and the harder they struggle the more he hangs on with all of his heart and soul. He remembers that the harder they fight the gentler he becomes, just as the angel had done as she held onto his line with only her thumb and one finger.

Jim travels about his way wearing his old overcoat, pants and hat, not only helping those in the back alleys and streets but testing those who claim to be true Christians yet many turn him away. Then he would come back later to tell them how wrong they were to judge a man for how he looked and to remind them all that what they do unto the least of them they have done unto the Lord himself. Then each and every winter he puts on the jolly old red suit and touches the lives of every child he can with hopes of filling them all with hopes and dreams and taking away their pain and heartache. Still to this day when he is alone, he finds himself whistling the tune Elijua whistled that special day to lead him to the porch of the old white house.

About the Author

James H. Pierce has been writing poetry and stories for most of his life.

He is a Structural Ironworker by trade, as he has followed in the foot steps of his father and grandfather, but his passion has always been the words that he has written and shared with others.

He has had poetry published in the USA and also throughout Europe, but his true passion is writing his stories for all to read. He has a collection of more than fifty stories of fiction and adventure that his followers have been reading throughout the years, these stories are soon to be published as well.

CPSIA information can be obtained at www.ICGtesting.com
Printed in the USA
LVOW072040080212

267794LV00001B/7/A